SHE'S STOLEN MY BABY

BERNICE BLOOM

NOTE TO READERS,

Hello – thank you so much for downloading 'She's Stolen My Baby', starring the magnificent Mary Brown. This is the twelfth book in the series about Mary.

If you have read all the previous books – thank you so much. If you fancy reading this but haven't read the others – no problem. They are all written so you can easily read them as stand-alone books.

At its heart, this novel is about what it means to become a parent, to face fears you didn't even know you had, and to find strength when you feel most vulnerable. It's a story about Mary and Ted, a couple who—like so many of us—are thrown into the beautiful, messy chaos of impending parenthood. But then their world is turned upside down.

There's a mystery at the heart of this story: a disappearance that shakes Mary and Ted to their core, forcing them to confront what they value most and what it means to truly protect the ones you love.

As you turn the pages, you'll find moments of lighthearted humour, a touch of suspense, and the unfolding of a relationship that is put to the ultimate test.

NOTE TO READERS,

Thank you for picking up this book. I hope you enjoy it x
Happy reading!

Bernice x

GRANDMA WARS

The late summer sun warmed Bridge Road as Mary stood before her bedroom mirror, surveying her latest attempt to accommodate her changing figure. The leopard print skirt had seemed a practical choice when she'd purchased it last week. Now, watching the fabric settle around her hips, she wasn't quite so certain.

'Oh, that looks nice,' said Charlie, surveying Mary's skirt.

'Thank you, kindly,' said Mary, spinning round to display the skirt in all its leopard print glory. 'It's got an elasticated waist, so it's one of the few items of pre-pregnancy clothing that I hope will take me through - expanding with my great girth. It's got a fitted sheer net underlay, so it's comfy.'

'And you look wonderful.'

'Thank-you. We both know I don't, I look like a hippo who killed a leopard and is wearing its clothing to taunt the rest of the leopard community, but the lie is much appreciated.'

'Behave. You are the prettiest hippo ever. You're glowing. Now, shall we brave the shops?'

Mary embraced her friend, and they strolled down Bridge

Road, accompanied by Elvis, her sprightly Cavapoo, fairly dancing along, urging his human companions to speed up.

The late morning air carried the scent of coffee and fresh-baked bread from the artisan bakery on the corner. Hampton Court bustled with its usual mix of tourists and locals. The palace grounds were visible in the distance, a reminder of the area's royal heritage.

The sun shone down as they walked along, sunglasses in place, smiles on their faces. They headed towards the little vintage shop, which housed the most curious clothes and jewellery. As they passed an antique furniture shop, Mary caught a glimpse of movement in the window's reflection - a man turning away too quickly. When she looked back, there was only the usual cluttered display of Victorian mirrors and aged dressing tables.

Their destination was the vintage boutique, its windows displaying an eclectic collection of clothes and jewellery. Charlie, with her tiny waist and endlessly long legs, could browse the clothing rails while Mary intended to focus on accessories.

As they approached the boutique, a car drove past and beeped its horn.

'Do you recognise him?' asked Charlie.

'No, perhaps he's remarking on our luminous beauty.'

'Could be,' said Charlie, doubtfully.

A young man on a bike cycled passed soon afterwards. 'Nice!' he shouted. 'Very nice indeed.'

'Why's everyone suddenly so keen on us?' asked Charlie.

'It could be Elvis. He's so beautiful; people always feel the need to tell me how lovely he is.'

The two women walked past the butcher's shop and waved merrily. Hampton Court was like Trumpton—everyone waved at each other and engaged in light chatter whenever they passed. The butcher smiled warmly, then stopped mid-wave, mouth wide open. His face bore the most peculiar expression.

'Something in the air today,' said Charlie, as Elvis found himself a very public spot and crouched down…his back legs shaking as he performed the ritual of every walk. Mary pulled out a poo bag and bent over to collect the rather unpleasant mess.

'Holy fuck!' shouted Charlie.

'What? I have to clear it up. You've seen me clear up after him before.'

'No - ah. Christ. I can see everything. What the hell? I can see when you last waxed, woman.'

Mary looked down. The leopard-print skirt had rolled up and was scrunched around the waistband. Just the diaphanous underskirt remained in place. She was exposing herself to everyone.

'What the hell? Why didn't you tell me sooner?'

'I told you as soon as I saw it.'

'Christ.'

Mary stood, pulling, stretching and trying to manipulate the material back into its rightful place.

'You couldn't see everything, could you? Not really?'

'You have a mole on your bikini line, and you need to get it checked out.'

'Great. You're not being very reassuring.'

'At least you had knickers on. They were pink with lace around the legs.'

'Brilliant. Absolutely bloody brilliant. My life is over. I'll have to move abroad and start a new life in Devon or somewhere.'

'Na, no point. The news will have travelled down there by now.'

'OK, Poland. I'm going to Warsaw to live.'

. . .

THE REMAINDER of the afternoon passed in a blur of mortification and half-hearted attempts at retail therapy. By late afternoon, Mary had almost convinced herself that the incident would soon be forgotten. Almost.

It wasn't until later that evening that the full consequences of her inadvertent exposure became apparent. She was in the bedroom, getting ready for an evening out. Her leopard print skirt was scrunched up in the bin while she stepped into a voluminous maxi dress that couldn't possibly ride up anywhere. She might look like she was wearing a tent, but at least she could cling onto the scraps of her dignity that were left.

'You've dropped that skirt in the bin,' said Ted, lifting it out.

'No, put it back. I'm throwing it away,' said Mary.

'Why? It's lovely.'

'I'm not saying.'

'Oh, OK.'

'If you must know, I had a nightmare today. It rode up, leaving me naked in the street.'

'Oh, *that* was the skirt, was it?'

'What do you mean - *'that* was the skirt, was it'?'

'Don't worry, angel. Bob said you looked very nice in your little pink knickers.'

'What are you talking about? Bob? Who's Bob?'

'The butcher. I popped in there earlier, and he said Rick in the antique shop saw you walking around in a see-through skirt, so Bob went to the window and looked out.'

'Oh God. I saw him looking. I can't believe they were sending each other messages. You have to be joking. Please tell me you're joking.'

'Yes, I'm joking. Got you there, didn't I?'

'You're not joking, are you?'

'No, I'm not, love. Everyone saw. Now - come on, we have

a dinner to attend and news to share about the rest of our lives.'

'OK. I'll come to the dinner tonight, but then I'm moving to Poland. Our baby will be born there and will be called Tomasz or something. I can't live in this country for a moment longer after what happened today.'

THE COUPLE WERE PREPARING to head out to dinner that evening with Mary's mum, Rosie, and Ted's mum Edna, to give them the exciting news that Mary was pregnant. Telling them the news was complicated by three things: firstly, Rosie already knew. Mary and Ted had told her on a recent trip to Paris. Secondly, in the interests of familial harmony, Rosie had agreed to pretend it was as much a surprise to her as to Ted's mum. Thirdly, and most significantly: Rosie was terrible at lying and was likely to cock the whole thing up by revealing that she knew all along.

'Come on then,' said Mary. 'Let's see how this all pans out.'

THE CANDLES FLICKERED on the table at Chez Pierre, casting a warm glow over the crisp white tablecloths and gleaming silverware. Mary sat ramrod straight, her napkin twisted into a tiny noose in her lap.

Did the butcher really see her waddling down the road in her pants? Christ, poor guy. No one should have to see that. 'So was it just Rick and Bob?' she whispered to Ted while, across the table, Rose and Edna beamed at them with the intensity of high-powered searchlights.

'A couple more guys saw, but nothing to worry about. Just focus on what we are doing here, and everything will be OK.'

'Oh God. I'm definitely buying a house in Poland. It's the only way forward.'

Ted kissed her lightly on the head. 'Are you going to tell them, or shall I?'

'What? About me buying a place in Warsaw?'

'No, you banana. About the whole pregnancy thing.'

'Oh, I see - yes, I will,' said Mary, clearing her throat and trying to concentrate.

'Mum, Edna, we have some news—'

'You're pregnant!' Rose shrieked, loud enough to make the neighbouring diners jump. 'I knew it! A grandmother always knows.'

Mary glanced at Ted. They had been through this so many times and rehearsed the routine as if they were going to perform it at the Olympics. Rosie was supposed to adopt a look of surprise and delight.

'Oh, sweetie,' Rosie said, reaching across to pat Mary's hand. 'You've been glowing all evening. I knew straight away that the two of you were expecting. It must be lovely for Edna to find out.'

Rosie gave Edna a withering smile.

'I knew too,' said Edna. 'Yep - I knew.'

Mary sat and watched in amazement as both grandmothers-to-be launched into a rapid-fire volley of questions, their voices overlapping in a dizzying cacophony.

'When are you due?' 'Have you picked a doctor?' 'Oh! We need to plan the baby shower!' 'What about names? Please tell me you're considering family names.'

'Whooahh... we haven't made any plans or chosen any names yet - we are coming to terms with it ourselves. We just wanted you both to know before anyone else, and we wanted to tell you both at the same time.'

'Right,' said Rosie, standing up so abruptly that her chair teetered dangerously. 'I have something for you.' She rummaged into her handbag, which was so deep that her entire arm appeared to disappear into its depths.

'Aha!' she exclaimed triumphantly, producing an antique silver rattle with a flourish. 'Family heirloom,' she announced, her eyes gleaming with triumph. 'Used by generations of our family.'

Rosie began to tell the tale of the rattle's extensive family history as Edna's eyes narrowed to slits.

'Why did you bring a rattle? You've only known about the pregnancy for five minutes.'

'Like I said - I just knew. A mother always knows.'

'OK, well, I have a gift, too,' said Edna, her fingers flying across her smartphone screen with the speed and precision of a concert pianist. 'I've just ordered you the BabySense Ultra Plus monitor. It tracks breathing patterns, heart rate, sleep cycles, and can even predict your child's future career path based on their gurgling patterns.'

Ted choked on his water, not sure whether to be impressed or depressed by this battle of the mums. 'Wow, Mom. That's... something.'

Mary nudged him. 'Quick,' she hissed. 'Change the conversation before they start arm-wrestling.'

As the evening progressed, the competition escalated until it reached staggering heights. Rose regaled them with tales of her superior child-rearing skills, miming changing nappies with her napkin.

'And that, my dears, is how you avoid the dreaded 'poop explosion," she finished with a flourish, just as the waiter arrived with their main course.

Edna countered by rattling off statistics from obscure parenting journals. 'Did you know that babies who listen to whale songs in utero are 72% more likely to excel at underwater basket weaving?'

'You need to put the baby on the waiting list for Prodigy Preschool,' Edna announced.

Rose scoffed. 'Preschool? Nonsense! I'll be providing full-time childcare. We'll focus on the classics–Homer, Shakespeare, advanced calculus.'

'Homer in the original Greek, I presume?' Ted mumbled into his crème brûlée.

While the group discussed potential educational approaches for their future child, a prickle of unease crawled up Mary's spine. Her gaze drifted to the corner of the restaurant, where it locked onto a pair of intense, dark eyes.

A man was hunched over a half-empty glass, his weathered face partially obscured by shadows and a day's stubble. His salt-and-pepper hair was dishevelled as if he'd repeatedly run his hands through it. There was something vaguely familiar about the sharp angle of his jaw and the deep creases around his eyes, but Mary couldn't quite place him.

There was something unsettling about the intensity of his gaze, something familiar yet foreign.

Beside him, a woman with ash-blonde hair pulled into a severe bun leaned in close, whispering urgently. Her thin lips were pressed into a tight line, and her fingers drummed an agitated rhythm on the table. Despite her companion's apparent distress, the man's gaze remained fixed on Mary and Ted's table.

Something about him tugged at her memory, like a half-forgotten dream. He was watching them intently, his gaze sharp and unsettling.

'Ted,' she whispered, leaning across the table, 'that man over there keeps staring at us. Do you think we know him from somewhere?'

Ted casually glanced over his shoulder, his brow furrowing slightly. 'I don't recognise him. But he seems interested in us. Want me to say something?'

Mary shook her head, forcing a smile. 'No, it's probably nothing. Let's just enjoy our dinner.'

But as the evening wore on, she couldn't shake the feeling of being watched. Whenever she looked up, those dark eyes were fixed on her, filled with an emotion she couldn't quite place. When she stood up to go to the toilet, she noticed the man's hand clenched tightly around a book of poetry, his knuckles white with tension.

'Perhaps he's waiting for you to take your skirt off?' said Ted when Mary returned.

'Ha, ha, ha. I'm too tired to think of a clever comeback.'

'Come on, let's get you home.'

As they waited for their cars outside the restaurant, Edna and Rose continued their enthusiastic planning.

'Come over this weekend. I'll show you how to puree organic vegetables into baby food,' Rose cooed.

'Actually,' Edna interjected, 'I was thinking of taking Mary shopping for maternity clothes. I know a wonderful boutique.'

Ted helped Mary into the car and then turned to their mothers. 'Thanks for dinner and all your... creative ideas. We'll be in touch about those weekend plans.'

As they drove away, Mary let out a long breath. 'Well, that was...'

'A preview of the next 18 years?' Ted supplied.

Mary groaned, then chuckled despite herself. 'At least the baby will have the most over-prepared, overly competitive grandmothers in history. Do you think they'll battle to see who gets to be in the delivery room?'

Ted grinned. 'My money's on your mum.'

They laughed together, allowing the stress of the evening to melt away. Neither of them noticed the dark sedan that pulled out behind them, following at a discreet distance.

Neither of them had any idea how difficult the sedan driver would make their lives over the next year.

TED SHUT THE DOOR, switched on the lights, and kicked his shoes off while Mary flopped onto the couch, the silver rattle still clutched in her hand. She examined it closely, tracing the intricate engravings with her finger. 'You know, despite all the craziness, this is beautiful,' she said.

Ted sat beside her, putting an arm around her shoulders. Mary leaned into him, sighing. 'I just hope we can maintain some semblance of control over our parenting choices.'

'We will. I'll make sure of it.'

'Ted,' she said slowly, 'I can't stop thinking about that man in the restaurant... the one staring at us. Are you sure you didn't know him from somewhere? He looked familiar to me. It was really strange.'

Ted frowned. 'I don't think so. I think he was staring because he was drunk.'

Mary shook her head, struggling to articulate the sense of unease she felt. ' He seemed to look right through me. I'm probably just being paranoid because I'm pregnant, and my hormones are up the spout, but he freaked me out.'

'Hey,' Ted said gently, giving her a squeeze, 'it's been a crazy night. Your mom and mine turned a simple dinner into 'Grandma Gladiators: Extreme Edition.' It's no wonder you're feeling a little on edge.'

Mary nodded, trying to shake off the lingering discomfort. 'You're right. It's probably nothing.'

As if on cue, both their phones chimed simultaneously. They exchanged a wary glance before checking the messages.

'Oh, for crying out loud,' Ted groaned. 'My mum's sent us

a link to a website for homeschooling. I don't think we'll be doing any of that.'

Mary burst out laughing. 'That's nothing. My mum just texted to ask if we've considered hiring a professional baby-namer. She's worried we might 'saddle the poor dear with something awful''

They dissolved into giggles, the absurdity of it all finally overcoming their stress and worry.

Later that night, as Mary went to close the bedroom curtains, she looked out of the window, the ancient silver rattle cool against her palm. The street outside was quiet, but somewhere in the darkness, she sensed watching eyes. Like her wayward skirt, like the competing grandmothers, like the mysterious stranger - everything seemed to be slipping beyond her control.

'Ted,' she said slowly, 'that man in the restaurant…'

'Hey, stop worrying. I'm here. Nothing can happen to you.'

Neither of them noticed the dark sedan that cruised past their house, its driver's face illuminated briefly by the glow of a mobile phone screen.

'MORNING SICKNESS MAYHEM'

Mary stood before the bathroom mirror, applying a final coat of lipstick with the precision of a neurosurgeon. Today was her big presentation to the board to pitch for the role of marketing manager of the DIY and gardening centre where she'd been working since time began. She'd always wanted to get her hands on a marketing role and had taken on the responsibility of raising the gardening centre's profile at every opportunity.

It was quite annoying that the job was finally being advertised now, when she was pregnant. She'd been angling after this role for years...always throwing her hat into the ring for all marketing-type activities. She'd decorated David Beckham's Christmas tree and organised trips for children, a dating service and even a trip to the centre from Rick Astley.

Things hadn't always gone according to plan, and - admittedly - there had been some terrible errors in which she'd drifted a little too closely to the edges of legality and morality - but she'd been there every time.

She smoothed down her blazer, took a deep breath, and gave her reflection a confident nod.

'You've got this,' she told herself. 'Nothing can stop you today.'

As if on cue, her stomach lurched. Mary's eyes widened in horror.

'Oh no. No, no, no. Not now.'

She barely made it to the toilet before the contents of her breakfast made a surprise reappearance.

Ted appeared in the doorway, his tie askew and a look of concern on his face. 'Honey? You okay?'

Mary lifted her head, her perfectly applied makeup now smeared. 'Do I look okay?' she croaked.

Ted winced as he looked at his wife's pale face. 'Mum sent me some old wives' remedies for morning sickness. I'll whip something up.'

Before Mary could protest, he dashed off to the kitchen. The sounds of clattering pots and slamming cabinets echoed through the apartment.

'Oh God,' Mary groaned, unsure whether it was morning sickness or dread of Ted's culinary attempts that led to another lurching feeling in her stomach.

Fifteen minutes later, Ted reappeared, proudly bearing a tray. 'Alright, we've got burnt toast. Don't look at me like that - apparently the char helps settle the stomach. Some extra salty crackers because... well, salt, I guess? And a nice cup of ginger tea.'

Mary eyed the offerings warily. The toast looked like it had been excavated from the ruins of Pompeii, and the crackers glistened ominously in the bathroom light. She picked up the mug of tea, took a sip, and immediately recoiled.

'Ted, honey, did you put the entire ginger root in here?'

Ted's face fell. 'Is it too strong?'

'I think my tongue just went numb.' Mary set the mug

down and nibbled on a cracker, instantly regretting it as her mouth turned into the Sahara Desert.

'Look, this isn't working; I'll just take a paracetamol and go.'

'Are you sure you should go in?' Ted asked, hovering anxiously.

Mary squared her shoulders. 'Ted, I've been preparing for this presentation for months. A little nausea isn't going to stop me.'

AT THE DIY and gardening centre, she strode purposefully towards the conference room, a sea of coworkers parting before her. This was her moment. So she was pregnant and weepy, and worried about a strange man who was staring at her in the restaurant, and she might be sick at any moment... but none of that would stop her. She was destined to become the marketing manager of this fine establishment, and nothing would stop her from fulfilling her destiny.

She'd taken the precaution of stopping at the chemist on the way and bought a pair of sea-sickness wristbands that the pharmacist had sworn would cure her nausea. All would be fine as long as she could hold her sickness at bay for the duration of her presentation. Hopefully, the wristbands would help.

Mary breathed deeply and set up her presentation materials. Her colleague Sarah leaned in. 'Loads of luck today. You'll be brilliant. I'll come and catch you on your break later.'

Mary forced a smile. 'Thank you. See you later.'

The board members filed in, and Mary launched into her carefully rehearsed spiel. Despite her churning stomach, she was nailing it. Graphs were explained, projections were projected, and she even managed to land a joke about David

Beckham's house that got a chuckle from the usually stoic CEO.

And then, disaster struck just as she was building to her big finish. The sea-sickness wristbands, which had been growing uncomfortably tight, suddenly snapped open with the force of a rubber band. One flew across the room, narrowly missing the CFO's head. The other shot straight up, becoming entangled in the overhead projector and casting strange, undulating shadows across Mary's meticulously prepared slides.

For a moment, silence reigned. Then Mary cleared her throat, summoning every ounce of her professional demeanour. 'And that, ladies and gentlemen, is a perfect metaphor for how our new marketing efforts will shake up the centre.'

To her immense relief, laughter rippled through the room. The CEO even gave her an approving nod as he ducked to avoid the dangling wristband.

That evening, Mary collapsed into bed, surrounded by a fortress of crackers. Ted eyed the crumb-covered sheets with trepidation.

'Uh, honey? Don't you think you're going overboard with the cracker thing?'

Mary fixed him with a glare that could have curdled milk. 'Do not say another word about my crackers.'

Ted raised his hands in surrender and carefully picked his way through the crummy minefield to his side of the bed.

Mary's morning sickness evolved into an all-day affair as the weeks passed. Her heightened sense of smell turned the world into an olfactory minefield. The perfume she'd worn for years now made her gag. The scent of coffee, once her lifeblood, sent her sprinting for the nearest bathroom.

But amid the chaos, she found unexpected allies. The women's restroom at work became a secret society of expectant mothers and sympathetic colleagues. Mary bonded even more with Sarah and swapped horror stories with Janet from accounting about their weirdest cravings.

'I woke up at 3 am convinced I would die if I didn't have pickled beetroot. My husband had to drive to three different shops to find some.'

Mary nodded sagely, reaching into her purse to pull out a jar of gherkins. 'I get it. I've been carrying these around for a week. The smell calms me down.'

But the real highlight of pregnancy cravings came on a Saturday morning. Mary woke up, bracing herself for the usual wave of nausea. To her surprise, it didn't come. Instead, an odd smell caught her attention. She followed her nose, leading her to the laundry basket and, specifically, to a pair of Ted's old gym socks.

Ted found her there, inhaling deeply with a blissful expression. 'Uh, Mary? Honey? What are you doing?'

Mary looked up, her eyes shining. 'Ted, the smell of your feet is my miracle cure.'

Ted blinked, unsure whether to be flattered or alarmed. 'That's... great?'

Ted's gym socks became Mary's constant companions from that day forward. She tucked them into her purse, hid them in her desk drawer, and even pinned one inside her work apron.

At their next prenatal appointment, the doctor raised an eyebrow at the sock peeking out of Mary's bag. 'That's certainly a unique remedy. But hey, if it works, it works.'

As they left the clinic, Ted squeezed Mary's hand. 'You know, when I imagined starting a family, I never thought my foot odour would play such a crucial role.'

Mary laughed, leaning into him. 'Just wait until the cravings kick in really hard. It's just gherkins at the moment, but

I hear pregnant women can get pretty creative with their food combinations.'

'You're not going to start dipping pickles in peanut butter, are you?'

'Don't be ridiculous,' Mary scoffed while thinking that it did sound kind of good.

That night, as they lay in bed, Mary's hand rested protectively over her still-flat stomach where she imagined a tiny bump growing. She turned to Ted. 'You know, despite all the craziness—the nausea, the mood swings, the weird smells—I wouldn't trade this for anything.'

Ted smiled, pulling her close. 'Me neither. However, I might invest in some better air fresheners. Our house smells like a men's changing room.'

Mary chuckled, then suddenly sat up. 'Oh. I almost forgot to tell you. Remember that weird guy from the restaurant? The one who was staring at us?'

Ted nodded, frowning. 'The one who *you* thought was staring at us?'

'I saw him outside the shop yesterday. Just for a second, but... it was him.'

Ted sat up. 'Are you sure?'

Mary shrugged, trying to shake off the uneasy feeling. 'It's probably nothing. Just pregnancy brain making me paranoid. I didn't see him in the shop. I went outside, and he was just standing there, staring. Very odd.'

Later, as Ted's breathing settled into the rhythm of sleep, Mary lay awake, one hand still curved over her abdomen. Beyond their bedroom window, a shadow moved in the darkness.

'CRAVINGS AND CHAOS'

Ted was dreaming of peaceful, sandy beaches when a sharp elbow to his ribs jolted him awake. He blinked blearily at the alarm clock: 2:13 AM. Beside him, Mary sat up, her eyes wide and intense.

'Ted,' she whispered urgently. 'I need it.'

Ted emerged from his cocoon of sleep, blinking owlishly. 'What do you need?'

'The Rocky Road ice cream from Avanti's. The one with a complicated name.'

'We have ice cream in the freezer.'

'No. It has to be that Ultimate Nutty Marshmallow Avalanche Rocky Road. They sell it at Avanti's. You know - the place that's open 24 hours.'

Ted stared at her. 'You woke me up for ice cream at two in the morning?'

Mary's lower lip trembled. 'The baby needs it, Ted. Don't you want our child to be happy? Do you want the baby to be born shrouded in a sadness that never leaves? Is that what you want for your firstborn? Really?'

Ted sighed, already reaching for his trousers. 'Of course I don't. But I'm sure our child doesn't have taste buds yet.'

'Ted,' Mary said, her voice low and dangerous. 'Baby needs ice cream.'

Recognising the tone that brooked no argument, Ted shuffled out of the bedroom, car keys in hand. As he reached the front door, Mary called out, 'Oh, and can you get some gherkins, too? And maybe some peanut butter? Ooh, and hot sauce.'

Ted paused, one shoe on. 'Anything else? Perhaps a partridge in a pear tree?'

'Don't be silly,' Mary replied. 'Pears give me heartburn. A bag of ice cubes as well.'

The streets of Hampton Court lay silent under street lamps as Ted navigated his way to Avanti's. The fluorescent glare of the 24-hour shop created pools of harsh light in the car park. Inside, a solitary container of the coveted ice cream waited like a holy grail on the bottom shelf.

All he needed to get now were pickles, peanut butter, ice and hot sauce.

With a groan, he turned to the condiment aisle, only to find it woefully understocked. Desperation mounting, he approached the only member of staff in the shop. 'You wouldn't know where I could find some pickles, peanut butter, and hot sauce at this hour, would you?'

The man regarded Ted's ice cream with the knowing look of someone who had witnessed this particular parade before.

'First trimester?' he enquired.

Ted nodded wearily.

'Try Denny's in Surbiton for the more... eccentric requirements.'

. . .

Twenty minutes later, Ted pulled up to a dilapidated corner store. A flickering neon sign proclaimed 'DENNY'S: WE NEVER CLOSE (SERIOUSLY, THE LOCK'S BROKEN)'.

Denny's proved to be an establishment that time had forgotten, or perhaps deliberately avoided. Its proprietor, a weathered man who appeared to have catalogued every pregnancy craving since the Victorian era, didn't wait for Ted to speak.

'The expecting fathers' aisle is third on the left,' he announced. 'We've arranged it by trimester and craving intensity.'

Ted blinked. 'How did you-'

Denny finally looked up, his rheumy eyes twinkling. 'Son, I've been running this place for forty years. I can smell a desperate dad-to-be from a mile away. What'll it be? We got dill pickles, bread-and-butter pickles, pickle-flavoured potato chips, pickle-scented air freshener...'

Five minutes later, Ted staggered out of Denny's with a bag full of pickles, three kinds of peanut butter (creamy, crunchy, and something ominously labelled 'marshmallow surprise.'), and a bottle of hot sauce that came with a waiver form.

When he stumbled through the front door at 4:37 AM, he saw Mary constructing a tower out of cream crackers and Philadelphia.

His wife looked up, her face lighting up at the sight of the bag. 'Oh, Ted. You're my hero.' She paused, sniffing the air. 'How did you find all this?'

Ted handed over the bag. 'Don't ask. Just... enjoy.'

As Mary gleefully dug into her Nutty Marshmallow Avalanche Rocky Road, topping it with pickles and a drizzle of hot sauce, Ted collapsed onto the sofa. Did all men have this? Or was Mary just a little bit more insane than other wives?

The next few weeks would confirm Ted's feelings that Mary was - indeed - just a little more insane than other wives. The food combinations became increasingly bizarre, and Ted's ever-more-desperate quests to satisfy them meant their kitchen became a laboratory of culinary horrors that would have made even the most adventurous chef weep.

One particularly memorable evening, Ted returned home to find Mary elbow-deep in a mixing bowl, a manic gleam in her eye.

'Honey?' he ventured cautiously. 'What are you making?'

Mary looked up, flour streaking her cheek. 'Pizza.'

Ted relaxed slightly. Pizza sounded normal, safe even. 'Oh, that's nice. What toppings are you using?'

Mary's grin widened. 'Pineapple, pickles, and chocolate sauce.'

Ted felt his stomach lurch. 'That's... creative.'

'I know, right?' Mary exclaimed, oblivious to Ted's growing horror. 'Oh, and I need you to run to the shop. we are out of anchovies and marshmallows.'

Ted thought about walking straight out of the house again before thinking better of it. 'Sure. Anything else?'

Mary thought for a moment. 'Actually, yes. I've been reading about this fruit called durian. It smells like gym socks and tastes like heaven. Can you get some?'

Ted blinked. 'Durian? Mary, we live in the suburbs of southwest London, not Malaysia. Where am I supposed to find all these weird foodstuffs?'

Mary's lower lip trembled, her eyes filling with tears. 'But... but the baby wants it.'

'Sure, no problem,' he said, walking out to his car and preparing for another journey to another shop where the assistant would think he'd lost his mind. Where the hell did you even start when looking for a fruit that smelled of stale vomit?

On that occasion, Ted admitted defeat and returned with a coconut, which she ate with gusto. She appeared to forget that her husband had left intending to purchase an entirely different fruit.

The toll of nocturnal food quests began to manifest in Ted's professional life. His colleagues watched with increasing concern as he navigated client meetings in a sleep-deprived haze. The betting pool regarding his inevitable breakdown was conducted with British discretion, though Janet from Accounting maintained detailed spreadsheets of his decline.

The reality, when it came, was somehow both less dramatic and more bizarre. Ted shuffled into an important client meeting, dark circles under his eyes, his tie askew. His eyes began drooping as the client droned on about quarterly projections. His colleagues watched in horrified fascination as he slumped forward, face-planting directly into his open laptop.

Ted was gently escorted from the room, still muttering about sentient pickles and durian fruit, while his boss made a mental note to have a serious talk with him about work-life balance... and possibly the merits of noise-cancelling headphones for sleeping through pregnancy cravings.

As Ted recounted the day's humiliations to Mary that evening, she listened with sympathy and barely suppressed laughter. 'Oh, honey,' she said, patting his hand. 'I'm sorry you're having such a rough time.'

Ted sighed, leaning back on the couch. 'It's okay. I know it's not easy for you. I wish I could do more to help.'

Mary smiled, snuggling up against him. 'Are you kidding? Ted, you've been amazing. You've indulged every crazy craving, cleaned up every kitchen disaster, and never complained about my demand for obscure foodstuffs. You're a remarkable man, and the good news is that I can feel the cravings starting to fade already. Before long, we'll be happy parents and pickles and ice creams will be in our past.'

As they sat there, Mary's head on Ted's shoulder, the chaos of the past weeks seemed to fade away. The kitchen disasters, the late-night food quests, the office humiliations—all paled compared to the excitement of their journey together.

'I love you,' said Mary, stroking the small patch of hair that emerged from the top of Ted's shirt.

He kissed her head lovingly. 'I love you', too.'

'There is just one thing,' she said. 'I'm sorry about this, but I desperately need a fish burger made with rainbow trout caught in a mountain stream under a full moon, preferably coated with a unique sauce made with chillies rolled on the thighs of virgins.'

Ted stared at her for a long moment, then burst out laughing. 'You're joking, right?'

'If I weren't joking, would you have headed out in search of a moonlit mountain stream and a couple of virgins?'

'Of course, dear.'

ULTRASOUND SURPRISE

The fluorescent-lit corridors of Kingston Hospital stretched before them like an elaborate maze. Mary gripped Ted's hand as they followed the conflicting arrows, their footsteps echoing against the linoleum floors.

Mary had the sense of direction of cabbage at the best of times, but with cryptic signs leading them into remote corridors and dead ends, it felt more like a treasure hunt than a trip to the maternity unit at the local hospital.

"Are we heading in the right direction?' Mary asked Ted, studying a sign that unhelpfully indicated both 'Radiology' and 'Cafeteria' down the same corridor.

Ted consulted the hospital map with uncharacteristic uncertainty. Despite his usual navigational prowess, the architectural logic of the building eluded him.

'According to this, we should be in the ultrasound department. Perhaps we came in the other way? I don't really know.' Ted was usually a whizz with maps, able to find a location with the precision of a hawk.

They rounded another corner and nearly collided with a

harried-looking nurse with a head full of unruly blonde curls.

'Excuse me,' Mary called out as the woman manoeuvred around them. 'Could you tell us where maternity is? We've been walking around in circles forever. The baby will be born before we find the place.'

The nurse dropped her head, not making contact with either of them. 'Down this hall, first door on the left. The one with the picture of the stork carrying a baby on it.'

Then she trundled off at lightning speed, pushing her trolley ahead.

'Blimey. She wasn't very friendly,' said Mary.

The ultrasound room provided a welcome respite from the hospital corridor's harsh lighting. Dimmed overheads cast a gentle glow across the medical equipment, while the hum of machinery created an atmosphere of hushed anticipation.

Mary's heart raced as she stepped inside, her palms clammy against the doorframe.

A large machine loomed before them, its curved arm extending over a padded bed draped in crinkly paper. The monitor's blank screen seemed to stare back at her, holding secrets yet to be revealed. Mary's nostrils flared at the sharp tang of disinfectant, a scent that clung to the walls and made her stomach churn with nerves.

Her eyes darted around the room, taking in the glossy posters of smiling babies and cross-sectioned wombs. Each image made her breath catch in her throat. A lone chair sat in the corner, its vinyl cushion creaking as Mary lowered herself onto it, her fingers drumming an anxious rhythm on her thighs.

The gentle knock of the sonographer at the door sent a jolt through Mary's body.

The ultrasound technician was a cheery woman with a

name tag that read 'Joy :)'—yes, the smiley face was part of her official hospital ID. She greeted them with the enthusiasm of someone who'd poured espresso directly into their bloodstream.

'Mary and Ted Brown?'

At their nods, she beamed. 'Wonderful. I'm Joy, and I'll be your tour guide through the wonderful world of your womb today. Mary, if you could just hop up on the table here and lift your shirt, we'll get started. Ted, you can have a seat right here.'

As Mary settled onto the examination table, Ted lowered himself gingerly into the chair recently vacated by his wife. 'I'm not going to faint,' he assured Joy. 'I've been practising. I can now look at raw chicken without getting light-headed.'

But Joy seemed distracted, pressing buttons on the machine as if she'd never seen it before. A light flashed and Joy visibly relaxed. Then she pressed another button and the machine went quiet.

'Sorry,' she said. 'I don't think it's working properly.'

The nurse scrabbled around, looking through a sheet of notes, before pressing a button and seeing the light come on again. Mary noticed how much the woman's hand was shaking.

'Is everything OK?'

'Yes, it will be,' said Joy.

The machine began whirring. Mary glanced at Ted. Was the machine broken or was the nurse completely incompetent? It was hard to tell.'

The nurse squeezed gel onto Mary's tummy and pressed the transducer down with such force that it hurt. Mary gasped, but the nurse carried on. The room filled with a rapid whooshing sound, like tiny horses galloping underwater.

'Is that...?' Ted breathed, leaning forward.

'That's your baby's heartbeat.'

Mary felt tears prick her eyes. 'Oh, Ted, listen to that. It's the most beautiful sound I've ever heard.'

Ted nodded, momentarily speechless. Then, 'Although, is it supposed to sound quite so... gallopy? It's like there's a pack of horses in there.'

Joy didn't answer. Her eyes were fixed on the screen, her brow furrowed. Mary watched as Joy leaned in closer, moving the transducer with more focused precision.

'Is everything okay?' asked Mary.

'Hmm,' Joy murmured. 'I just need to check something. Excuse me for a moment.'

She stepped out of the room, clutching the notes that she'd been previously looking through, and leaving the transducer lying on Mary's stomach. Mary and Ted were left there in a stew of anxiety and confusion.

'What do you think is wrong? Is the baby okay? Oh God, what if it has two heads? Or no head? Or three legs?'

Ted pulled the chair in so it sat next to the bed and held Mary's hand reassuringly, though his own face had gone pale. 'I'm sure everything's fine,' he said. 'She doesn't really seem to know what she's doing though. Perhaps I should go and see whether I can find someone to help.'

Before Mary could respond, they heard muffled voices from the hallway. Joy's voice sounded tense.

An older male voice responded, sounding irritated. 'How long have you been working here? It's not that hard, but I'll come and take a look.'

Mary and Ted exchanged worried glances. Ted shrugged helplessly.

The door opened, and Joy returned, followed by a distinguished-looking man whose name tag proclaimed him to be 'Dr. Heggarty.'

'Mr. and Mrs. Brown. I apologise for the delay. Let me just check what's going on here,' said the doctor.

Mary's eyes widened. 'Is something wrong with the baby?'

Dr. Heggarty looked at the screen. 'Not at all. In fact, we have some exciting news for you.' He nodded to Joy, who looked at him blankly.

The doctor shook his head and took over the consultation.

'If you'll look at the screen,' he said, moving the transducer, 'you'll see... here's your baby's head... and here's the spine... and over here is... another head.'

The room went silent, save for the thunderous whooshing.

Ted leaned forward, squinting at the screen. 'I'm sorry, did you say another head? As in, our baby has two heads?'

Dr. Heggarty chuckled. 'No, Mr. Brown. Your baby doesn't have two heads. You're having two babies. Twins.'

Mary's jaw dropped. Ted's face went through a rapid series of expressions, cycling from confusion to shock to joy to abject terror.

'Twins?' Mary breathed. 'Are you sure?'

Ted stood up, swaying slightly. 'Twins,' he repeated, his voice faint. 'Two babies.'

Mary's eyes remained fixed on the ultrasound screen. In grainy black and white, she could see two distinct shapes.

'Twins,' Ted said again as if repeating it might somehow make it less overwhelming. 'we are having twins. Two babies. At the same time. How is that even possible?'

Dr. Heggarty raised an eyebrow. 'Well, Mr Brown, when a mummy egg and a daddy sperm love each other very much...'

'I know how it's possible,' Ted interrupted, his face flushing. 'I just meant... wow. Twins.'

Mary reached out and took his hand. 'We can do this,

right? I mean, it's just one more baby than we planned for. How hard can it be?'

Ted nodded, a goofy grin spreading across his face. 'Right. We've got this. We'll just need to double everything. Double the love, double the fun, double the...'

'Sleep deprivation?' the doctor supplied, helpfully.

'...joy,' Ted finished weakly.

As the doctor finished the ultrasound, pointing out tiny fingers and toes (there were so many toes), Mary and Ted fell into a dazed silence, their minds racing with the implications of their double bundle of joy.

Finally, wiping the gel from Mary's belly, the doctor handed them a strip of ultrasound photos. 'Here you go, Mom and Dad. These are the first pictures of your dynamic duo. Did you see where the nurse went?'

'No,' they chorused.

'I'll go and find her and get her to clear up. In the meantime - you're free to leave whenever you're ready.'

Mary and Ted left the ultrasound room in disbelief and excitement, clutching the precious photos like a lifeline. As they returned through the hospital's convoluted corridors, they began to process the magnitude of what they'd just learned.

'we are going to need a bigger car,' Ted mused. 'And probably a bigger house. And definitely a bigger savings account.'

Mary nodded absently, then suddenly stopped short. 'Oh no.'

Ted looked at her in alarm. 'What? What's wrong? Are you feeling okay? Is it the babies? Do you need to sit down?'

Mary shook her head. 'No, it's not that. I just realised... we have to tell our mothers.'

Ted's face drained of colour. 'Oh God. They're going to lose their minds over this. We'll be drowning in hand-knitted onesies and baby monitors.'

As they approached the hospital exit, still shell-shocked and muttering about the need to buy everything in pairs, neither noticed the intense gaze of a woman watching them closely. Her eyes followed them out the door, lingering on the ultrasound photos clutched in Mary's hand.

Once outside, Mary took a deep breath of fresh air. 'Okay. Twins. We can handle this. We must stay calm, plan, and maybe invest in a good coffee maker.'

As they walked towards the car, Mary thought she glimpsed a man who looked familiar. 'Is that the guy who was in the restaurant the other day?' asked Mary.

'Where? I don't see anyone.'

The man had gone. Perhaps she'd imagined it.

They drove away from the hospital, minds whirling with plans and to-do lists that seemed to grow exponentially by the second, neither noticed that they were being observed by an unnoticed figure—a woman whose intense gaze followed their progress, lingering on the ultrasound photos in Mary's hand.

As Mary and Ted reached their car, she withdrew a mobile phone and spoke three quiet words: 'It is twins.'

BACK IN THEIR CAR, blissfully unaware of wheels turning behind the scenes, Mary and Ted bantered back and forth, tossing around baby names.

'They should start with the same letter,' said Mary. 'You know - like Tessa and Timmy or something.'

'They sound like characters in a children's book. We can't do that to them.'

'I think it would be nice.'

'Na. Let's just pick two names we love. We don't have to turn them into Enid Blyton characters.'

'Simon and Susie?'

'No, stop it.'

'Abi and Andy.'

'Mary, I swear to God, you're not going to name the children as if they're in an episode of Noddy goes to the seaside. We need proper, majestic names, like Victoria and Richard.'

'No, we can't do that because then they'll be Vick and Dick.'

'Bertrand is a nice name.'

'Bertie Brown? Are you sure?'

'Blimey, this is harder than you realise, isn't it? What names do you like, but not bloody matching ones.'

'I like Daisy for a girl and Daniel for a boy.'

'Daisy is nice. Dan isn't bad, either. Or George. That's a lovely name.'

'Daisy and George? I quite like that.'

As they pulled into their driveway, Ted turned to Mary with a grin. 'You know what? We'll be happy we had twins when they're a bit older. They'll always have a special bond and someone to play with. I know it's going to be hard at first, but we'll do it together.'

Mary nodded, her hand resting on her belly. 'You're right. We've got this.'

MARY GATHERED her handbag and coat and followed Ted into the house. She eased herself onto the sofa and closed her eyes. Her insides were going that odd whirring thing they did before every bout of morning sickness. She was bracing herself for a quick run to the loo, when the doorbell rang.

'Did you invite someone over?'

Ted shook his head. 'No. Maybe if we are very quiet, they'll go away.'

The doorbell rang again, more insistently this time.

With a sigh, Ted went to answer the door. He opened it to

find a delivery man holding a large, elaborately wrapped package.

'Delivery for Mr. and Mrs. Brown,' the man said, consulting his clipboard.

Ted frowned. 'We didn't order anything.'

The delivery man shrugged. 'Hey, man, I just deliver 'em. I don't ask questions. Sign here, please.'

Ted signed and brought it inside. Mary looked at him curiously.

'What is it?'

'No idea.'

Cautiously, they unwrapped the package together. Inside was an antique wooden box, intricately carved with symbols neither of them recognised. Nestled within the box, on a bed of velvet, lay a silver rattle, identical to the one Mary's mother had given them.

A note sat atop the rattle, written in an elegant, old-fashioned script:

'For the twins. You have one rattle. Here is another.'

Mary and Ted stared at each other, a mixture of confusion and unease settling over them.

'Ted,' Mary said slowly. 'How does anyone know we are having twins? We haven't told a soul yet.'

'I don't know. Could it be from the hospital?'

'The hospital? They don't send gifts to everyone who's having a baby.'

'I know, but they are the only people who know we are having two babies.'

'They don't know about the rattle. This is really strange.'

As the sun set outside their window, casting a warm glow over the room, Mary and Ted sat in silence, the mysterious rattle lying on the table in front of them.'

'I'm worried about this,' said Mary. 'It's just weird.'

'I know. It's odd, but there's no point worrying.'

'Can you call the hospital to ask whether anyone else has been told? They wouldn't ring our parents or anything, would they?'

'No, of course not. I'm sure medical professionals are not allowed to tell anyone. In any case, they only found out that it was twins half an hour ago, at the same time that we found out about it.'

'I don't feel comfortable. Can you call them? It would make sense if mum somehow knew, and sent a second one. It's odd to be like this, and not have a clue.'

'Of course, said Ted, googling the number of the hospital's maternity unit.

Mary listened to her husband explaining the bizarre gift. She could tell from his reaction that they knew nothing about it.

Ted tried again, saying that someone knew, and the only people who could have told them were the hospital staff. He mentioned that Joy was their nurse. Ted was silent as he listened to the nurse's response. Then he thanked them and put the phone down.

'They said no one at the hospital would ever ring anyone, and the news hasn't even been formally put onto our file yet, so it hasn't come from them.'

'What about nurse Joy?'

'They didn't even seem to know who she was. I don't think she's very senior.'

'No. I don't think she knew what she was doing. Must have been her first day or something.'

'Yes. But the fact remains that no one outside that room was informed that we are having twins. Yet someone knew—someone who managed to deliver this gift with implausible speed.

THE MAN IN THE SHADOWS

Two weeks after the ultrasound revelation, Mary emerged from her doctor's surgery into the autumn sunshine. The brick buildings of Hampton Court High Street stretched before her, their Georgian facades catching the late morning light. All was well with the twins; they were growing well, she was healthy and the morning sickness was finally beginning to fade.

The street bustled with its usual mix of tourists and locals.

Mary smiled to herself. She was so lucky; she had two beautiful, healthy babies growing inside her, and the loveliest husband in the world.

She was in a world of her own when a flash of movement caught her eye. She looked up. The man who'd been watching her in the restaurant was across the street, partially hidden behind a newspaper stand. His presence sent a jolt of anxiety through her, dampening her earlier happiness.

Mary's steps faltered as she processed the implications. One sighting at the restaurant could be dismissed as imagination. A glimpse outside the hospital might be coincidence.

But this third appearance suggested something more calculated, more unsettling.

She quickened her pace, her hand instinctively settling over her abdomen. The cobblestones beneath her feet seemed to mock her attempts at haste, each step requiring more concentration than it should. The autumn wind carried fragments of conversations and the distant chime of church bells, but beneath these familiar sounds, she detected footsteps that matched her rhythm too precisely.

The route to her car took her past Creek Road, where scaffolding created shadows perfect for concealment. Mary considered ducking into Boots, losing herself among the aisles of vitamins and baby supplies, but the thought of being trapped inside made her chest tighten. She left the shop and walked up the road as fast as she could.

The touch on her shoulder came just as she reached the corner. Mary spun around, her cry of alarm catching in her throat.

'Mary?' Ted's concerned face replaced her fears of confrontation. 'What's wrong?'

Her eyes darted back to the newspaper stand, but the familiar figure had vanished. The space where he'd stood now held only a group of tourists consulting their phones.

'He was here again,' she said, her voice steadier than she felt. 'The man from the restaurant.'

Ted's expression hardened as he scanned the street, his arm coming around her shoulders. The gesture was protective rather than comforting, and Mary noticed how his gaze lingered on the shadows between buildings.

'That's three times now,' Ted said as they walked to their car. 'First the restaurant, then the hospital, now here. We should report this.'

'To whom?' Mary asked. 'We don't have proof, and I

haven't even seen his face clearly. They'll think I'm being paranoid.'

'Better paranoid than careless. Especially now.'

At home, Mary sat at their kitchen table, wrapped in the cardigan Ted had draped around her shoulders. The familiar space felt different somehow, as if the outside world's uncertainties had followed them in. Ted busied himself making tea, the domestic rhythm of spoons against cups a futile attempt at normalcy.

'Perhaps we should install security cameras,' he suggested, setting her cup down. 'Just to be safe.'

Mary traced the rim of her cup, considering their options. 'It's not just the sightings, Ted. It's everything. The rattles appearing moments after we learned about the twins. The way that nurse at the hospital wouldn't meet our eyes. Something feels... orchestrated.'

'Like we are being watched?'

'Like we are part of something we don't understand.'

Later that night, as Ted checked the locks for the third time, Mary stood at their bedroom window. The street below lay quiet, but somewhere in the darkness, she sensed watching eyes. The invitation sat on their bedside table, its golden lettering catching the lamplight. Two intertwined trees, she thought, like two intertwined fates.

Her hand rested on her stomach, where their twins grew, unaware of the mystery surrounding them. Whatever was happening, whatever this surveillance meant, she knew one thing with certainty: she would protect them, no matter what.

BELLY BUMP BLUNDERS

The morning light filtered through the bedroom curtains as Mary confronted her reflection, engaged in what she knew to be a futile battle with her pre-pregnancy jeans. Her expanding figure—accommodating two new lives— seemed to mock her efforts, gleefully resisting every tug and shimmy.

'Come on,' Mary grunted, sucking in her stomach as much as her twin-filled uterus would allow. 'Just... a little... more...'

With a final, heroic effort, she managed to pull the zipper up halfway. Triumph surged through her veins. She was doing it. She was defying the laws of physics and squeezing her pregnant body into her favourite jeans.

And then, with a sound like a champagne cork popping, the button gave up the ghost. It shot across the room with the velocity of a speeding bullet, ricocheted off the dresser, and scored a direct hit on the bedside lamp. The lamp wobbled precariously for a moment, then toppled over with a crash.

The small commotion sent Ted running into the room.

'What happened? Are you okay? Did your waters break? Is it time? Should I boil water? Why do people always say to boil water? What's the boiled water for?'

'Nothing to worry about. I'm just very, very fat.'

'No you're not. You're pregnant. Stop being horrible to yourself. What was the crash? The lamp's on the floor. Is everything OK?'

'No, Ted, everything is not OK. I can't get into my jeans.'

'That doesn't matter. Wear something else.'

'But I tried, and I committed 'jean-icide.'

'Jeanicide? That's quite funny.'

'Nope. Not funny.'

Ted looked from his wife's sad face to jeans stuck against her thighs, hugging them in much the same way that sausage casing hugs sausage meat. This wasn't the time to be flippant. He'd learned that over the past months.

'Oh, honey,' he said, pulling her close. 'I think it might be time to admit defeat and buy some maternity clothes.'

Mary's lower lip trembled. 'But I liked these jeans. They made my bum look good.'

Ted approached cautiously, as one might a wild animal. 'Your bum looks great in everything. But right now, I'm more concerned about getting you out of those jeans before they cut off your circulation and starve our child of oxygen.'

'OK,' said Mary reluctantly. 'Let's get maternity clothes, but you need to bear in mind that I'm very cross about this.'

'OK. Can I ask why?'

'The whole thing is hard, you know? It's like the babies are completely taking over. When I go out with the girls, I drink Earl Grey tea and come home early.

'That's not like me.

'I remember when I'd go out for a glass of wine and end up at a drag club in Cardiff two days later with some guy we met on the train. We'd bump into three blokes on a stag do and three members of a brass band complete with instruments and have a whale of a time.

'I'm the woman who was arrested on her hen weekend, remember. It feels like everything has changed.

'I know I should be grateful to be healthy and carrying twins, but my life is so different from the way it was a year ago. Maternity clothes feel like another step away from the old me.'

'IT WON'T BE SO BAD,' said Ted as they climbed out of the car and walking towards the maternity clothing shop.

'I bet it will. Pregnant women all look awful. They look so pleased with themselves. I don't want to be one of them. I liked being me the way I was. Can't I just be me, like I was, but with babies?'

'Once the babies have been born, that's exactly what you'll be like.'

'Yes, and all these maternity clothes will go straight in the bin, OK?

'No problem. We'll burn them once the pregnancy is over.'

Mary stomped into the shop, in the manner of a teenager being taken to parents' evening, emanating anger and frustration at the unfairness of life.

But she was in for something as a surprise.

There were racks of comfortable-looking stretchy trousers and gorgeous flowing tops everywhere. This place was a revelation. There were no sailor dresses or fussy floral dresses with lacy collars, just lovely, comfortable clothing.

Mary had been overweight for years and was well-used to failing to fit into anything in a boutique.

Here she was in a fat girl's paradise.

The place was awash with dresses that weren't fitted,

tunic tops that covered every lump and bump, and elastic waistbands that screamed, 'I will fit you, even if you are the size of a blue whale.'

'I know it's not very fashionable, but it'll be comfortable, and it's only for a few months,' said Ted.

'I LOVE IT,' Mary growled, picking up a pair of trousers. 'I mean - take a look at these. That waistband could stretch around a medium-sized family car. They are magnificent. Truly magnificent.'

'Oh good,' said Ted, slightly confused about the sudden change of mood.

As Mary ventured deeper into the store, she found herself ensnared in a labyrinth of stretchy fabric. Racks of leggings and yoga pants, rows of jogging bottoms.

'What are jeggings?' asked Ted.

'They are jeans without buttons that fly off. Once again - magnificent.'

It took only minutes for Mary to emerge from the clothing jungle with her arms full of maternity items. She headed for the fitting rooms, determined to find something - anything - that had the combined qualities of fit and comfort. Never again would she walk up the street to discover that her skirt had rolled up to her waist. Bob the butcher would have to find something else to stare at from now on.

The first few items that Mary slipped into were disappointing. The pants either gaped awkwardly or squeezed in all the wrong places. The tops either made her look like she was wearing a deflated hot air balloon or clung so tightly it was practically illegal.

Finally, she tried on a flowing top that seemed promising. It draped nicely over her bump and didn't make her feel like she was wearing a tent. They had one in a lovely turquoise colour and one in pink. She was getting them both. She bought leggings, a pair of jeggings and two dresses…all of them offering her the sort of comfort that thrilled her little heart.

'Why didn't we come here ages ago?' she said.

'You didn't want to. I suggested it a few times, but you said you didn't want to come.'

'I should have been coming here for years.'

They left the store with clothes that Mary hoped would see her through the rest of her pregnancy without any more wardrobe malfunctions. Ted had even suggested buying the items she liked best in a few sizes bigger so that she could be just as comfortable in the later stages of pregnancy.

'I'll never be that big,' Mary had said.

Ha! Mary had grossly underestimated how big a woman gets when carrying twins. As the weeks passed her figure expanded beyond all the clothes she'd bought. Indeed, her stomach grew beyond everything. It seemed to have a mind of its own, knocking over plants and gardening tools and bumping into unsuspecting customers.

One slight movement of her hip against the display table, and suddenly hundreds of seed packets fluttered to the floor in elegant disarray. Walking past the mountain of sprays too quickly and they would all come thundering down to the floor.

Picking things up was very tricky, her advanced state of pregnancy having turned simple bending into an Olympic-worthy event.

The number of times she'd almost exposed herself to a startled audience of garden ornaments and their equally surprised browsers was too many counts. The gnomes, at least, had the decency to maintain their frozen smiles.

. . .

BERNICE BLOOM

'It's awful,' Mary explained that evening as she and Ted drove off to attend their first birthing class.

'You know, your pregnancy seems to involve a great number of incidents in which you expose yourself,' he said. 'Is this something you're doing on purpose?'

'Er...no. The last thing I want is for anyone to see this dreadful body, but my dreadful body seems to be very keen to come out and see everyone.'

'Stop being so hard on yourself. Anyway, you haven't got long to go now until maternity leave starts.'

'I guess not. I wish I didn't have to go to fat women's club tonight though.'

'It's not 'fat women's club' it's a NCT course about pregnancy and childbirth.'

'I know: gross.'

'It's supposed to be the woman who wants to go and the man who gets dragged along. You've got no interest at all, and I've been looking forward to it.'

'Why don't you go, and report back on what they say?'

Maybe I should have the baby for you as well?'

'Oh God - could you?'

The instructor, a chirpy woman named Sunshine (because of course she was). She clapped her hands to get everyone's attention and drag them from the disappointing collection of herbal teas and dried up oat cakes that passed for 'snacks'.

'Alright, mummies and daddies. Let's start with some introductions. Why don't we all go round the room and introduce ourselves? Tell the group something interesting about you...'

'Oh God,' Mary whispered to Ted. 'Can't we just get on with the meeting? I don't give a toss about whether Majorie has a horse or whether Graham likes red socks.'

'Just be normal,' said Ted, nudging his wife affectionately. 'And don't say anything silly.'

The room rang out with the sounds of people offering little insights into their personalities.

'I'm a teacher.'

'I have a dog called Lionel.'

'I love gardening.'

Ted offered the news that Mary was expecting twins.

'Congratulations,' said Sunshine. 'Now tell us something about you, Mary.'

'I'm a mermaid,' said Mary. Sunshine smiled, Ted dropped his head into his hands, and Amanda who likes gardening said 'Gosh.'

'When you say 'mermaid'…' said a woman in a big coat.

'Yep - mermaid. You know. Half fish.'

'She's joking,' said Ted. 'She's not half-fish, she won't be laying eggs. No fins. Nothing fishy at all.' His voice rang with exasperation.

'Oh, I see,' said Sunshine. 'Very good. Very funny. Who's next?'

FROM INTRODUCTIONS, the group progressed to squatting exercises.

'You just need to squat heavily on the ball and sit there,' said Sunshine.

'Oh, I'll be good at this,' said Mary. 'I might play my joker.'

'It's very useful to do this regularly. It will help prepare your bodies for the miracle of birth.'

'I've got this,' said Mary, lowering herself into a squat. She perched comfortably on the ball, moving her hips around, as instructed.

The rest of the women in the class did it, too, with varying degrees of success.

'I wonder whether I can take my feet off the ground.'

'No,' said Ted.

'Look,' Mary wheeled her arms around as she fought to keep her balance.

'Put your feet down or you'll fall,' said Ted.

'You're no fun.'

'It's not supposed to be fun.'

'I know. That's the problem. Pregnancy should be special, glorious, wonderful and - yes - fun. But it's all so joyless and serious.'

'It won't be much fun if you fall off the ball while you're messing around...oh God...'

It was all highly predictable, but nevertheless alarming, when it happened.

Mary toppled backwards, crashing into Ted who'd moved in to try and catch her. He, in turn, fell into the couple behind them, while the ball shot from underneath Mary. Within seconds, the entire class had fallen like dominoes, a tangle of pregnant bellies and flailing limbs.

Sunshine, to her credit, maintained her peppy demeanour. 'Excellent bonding exercise,' she said. 'Now, let's try something else.'

That 'something else' was swaddling practice. Ted volunteered to demonstrate, determined to prove his worth as a future father. He approached the plastic baby doll with the intensity of a bomb disposal expert facing a particularly tricky explosive.

'Okay,' he muttered, unfolding the swaddling blanket. 'I've got this. It's just like wrapping a burrito, right? A very fragile, screaming burrito.'

What followed was a master class on how not to swaddle a baby.

Mary, watching from her mat, couldn't contain her laughter. 'Oh, Ted,' she gasped between giggles, 'I think you're supposed to keep the head on the baby. I might be wrong, but I always pictured the baby being alive at the end of it.'

Ted grinned sheepishly. 'You can't have everything, Mary. It's swaddled; no one said anything about keeping it alive.'

As the weeks passed and Mary's due date approached, the Browns settled into a routine of doctor's appointments, nursery preparations, and increasingly frequent bathroom breaks. They thought they were prepared for anything.

They were wrong. No pregnant woman is ever prepared for anything.

Mary was on maternity leave when it happened. She had popped into work to say hello to her colleagues when she felt a sudden, sharp pain. She paused, taking a deep breath, then continued. But the pain came again, stronger this time.

She doubled over, clutching her belly. Her colleague, Sarah, was at her side in an instant. 'Mary? Are you okay?'

Mary looked up, her eyes wide with excitement and terror. 'I think... I think it's time.'

The shop erupted into chaos. Someone called Ted. Someone ran to get blankets and a pillow from the garden furnishings section of the store. Someone else ran to make hot, sweet tea. Mary lay on her side, her arms wrapped around her bump while agonising pains shot through her.

Ted arrived in record time, skidding into the office like an F1 driver. 'I'm here. Where's my wife?'

Mary, who had been calmly timing her contractions while her coworkers ran around like headless chickens, waved at him. 'Over here. Ready to have a baby?'

The journey to the hospital unfolded beneath a sky heavy with autumn clouds. Each contraction marked time like a metronome, growing steadily more insistent. Ted navigated London's streets with uncharacteristic focus, his usual running commentary replaced by concerned glances.

Mary's contractions were coming faster now, each wave

of pain causing her to grip the dashboard tightly and scream obscenities at her husband. Ted's knuckles were white on the steering wheel, his eyes darting between the road and his wife's face.

'we are almost there, honey. Just hold on.'

Mary nodded, unable to speak as another contraction washed over her.

As they pulled into the hospital parking lot, Mary's waters broke. The sudden gush caught them both by surprise and for a moment, they stared at each other in shock.

'Oh my God, Ted,' Mary whispered, her eyes wide. 'This is happening. Also - sorry about the car seat.'

Ted sprang into action, his movements frantic but purposeful. He helped Mary out of the car, supporting her weight as they made their way to the entrance.

The delivery suite housed its own universe, where time measured itself in breaths and heartbeats rather than minutes and hours. Mary's world narrowed to the rhythm of contractions and the steady presence of Ted beside her.

As the contractions intensified, Mary's grip on Ted's hand tightened. She let out a low moan, the pain unlike anything she had ever experienced. Ted winced but didn't pull away, his presence a steadying anchor.

'You're doing very well, Mrs. Brown,' the nurse encouraged. 'Just a few more pushes.'

Mary nodded, gathering her strength. With each push, she felt she was being torn apart and put back together. The pain was overwhelming, but beneath it was a current of determination and love so strong it took her breath away.

Finally, with a cry that seemed to come from the very depths of her being, Mary gave one last monumental push. The room filled with the sound of a baby's first cry, strong and indignant.

'It's a boy!' the doctor announced, holding up the squirming, red-faced infant.

Tears streamed down Mary's face as she caught her first glimpse of her son. He was perfect - tiny and wrinkled and absolutely beautiful. Ted cut the umbilical cord with shaking hands, his eyes never leaving his son's face.

'Hello George,' he said.

But there was no time to rest. Within minutes, Mary felt the urge to push again. The second delivery was quicker but no less intense. Mary brought their daughter into the world with a final, exhausted effort.

The room was filled with the cries of two newborns, a duet that made Mary's heart swell with love. As the nurses cleaned and checked the babies, Mary and Ted shared a look of pure wonder and joy.

In the quiet aftermath, as London's evening settled beyond their window, Mary and Ted absorbed the reality of their expanded family. Their son displayed Ted's distinctive profile, while their daughter's delicate features hinted at Mary's side of the family.

'Daisy and George,' Ted said softly, touching each tiny hand in turn.

Mary watched their sleeping faces, marvelling at how their world had shifted to accommodate these new lives. All her earlier fears about losing herself seemed to fade in importance. She hadn't lost anything—she'd gained an expanded version of herself, one that included being mother to these remarkable beings.

'We did it,' Mary whispered, her voice hoarse from exertion. 'They're here. They're really here.'

Ted leaned down and kissed her forehead, his own tears

mingling with hers. 'You were amazing,' he said, his voice thick with emotion. 'I love you so much.'

The nurses brought George and Daisy over, placing them gently in Mary's arms. As she looked down at their tiny faces, Mary felt a love so profound it almost hurt.

'Hello,' she cooed, her voice soft and full of wonder. 'We've been waiting so long to meet you.'

Ted perched on the edge of the bed, his arm around Mary, his other hand gently stroking his daughter's cheek. The babies blinked up at them, their eyes unfocused but seeming to take in their parents' faces.

'It's Daisy and George,' said Ted. 'The names suit them.'

'Daisy and George,' said Mary. 'I feel like the luckiest woman in the world.'

As TWILIGHT DEEPENED outside their window, neither parent noticed the dark sedan that pulled slowly past the hospital, its driver studying the maternity ward with careful attention. Nor did they see the elegant figure who stood in the hospital garden, looking up at their window with an expression of intense interest.

DAISY & GEORGE

In the hushed sanctuary of the delivery suite, Mary cradled her newborns, each breath a prayer of gratitude. Daisy and George slept peacefully in her arms.

'They're so beautiful,' Ted murmured, his voice filled with awe. 'I can't believe they're ours.'

Mary nodded, unable to speak past the lump in her throat. She had never felt so complete, so utterly content. The world outside the delivery room ceased to exist - all that mattered was here, at this moment, with her family.

A nurse approached, her smile warm and reassuring. 'Would you like me to take the little girl for her routine check-up? Give you three a moment to bond?'

Mary hesitated, maternal instinct warring with medical protocol. Through the fog of fatigue, she caught a glimpse of something in the nurse's eyes—a flash of intensity that seemed out of place. But the moment passed, dismissed as new-mother anxiety.

The nurse smiled and gently touched Mary's arm. 'It'll just be a few minutes,' the nurse promised, her voice soft and understanding.

Mary nodded, carefully passing her daughter to the nurse.

'I'll be back very soon,' the nurse said as she wheeled tiny Daisy away.

Mary's eyes followed the nurse until she was out of sight.

The minutes after Daisy's departure stretched like elastic, each second drawing out longer than the last. Mary drifted between consciousness and sleep, George's warmth against her chest the only constant.

Through the haze of post-delivery fatigue, she caught a glimpse of a familiar silhouette in the hallway. For a moment, her breath caught. It was him - the man who had been watching her. He stood there, just for a second, his eyes meeting hers with an intensity that sent a chill through her despite the warm hospital room.

Mary blinked, and he was gone. She shook her head, trying to clear the fog from her mind. 'Ted,' she murmured, 'I think I saw...'

But sleep was already pulling her under, the image of the man fading like a half-remembered dream.

Ted leaned in, pressing a kiss to Mary's temple. 'You've given me the greatest gift, Mary,' he whispered. 'Thank you for our beautiful family.'

As they sat together, marvelling at the miracle of their son and eagerly awaiting the return of their daughter, Mary and Ted felt more love for one another than they had ever felt before.

Ted leaned in to kiss her forehead, gently stroking their son's cheek. 'You did it, supermum. I just stood there and tried not to pass out.'

They sat together, basking in the glow of new parenthood, until the doctor returned a short while later.

'Alright, let's look at those beautiful babies of yours,' he said cheerfully.

SHE'S STOLEN MY BABY

Mary and Ted exchanged a confused look. 'But... the nurse just took our daughter for a check-up,' Mary said, her voice tinged with uncertainty. 'Our son is here.'

The doctor's smile faltered, his brow furrowing. 'What nurse? We haven't sent anyone in to take either baby.' He paused, glancing at the clipboard in his hands. 'Let me just check with the nursing staff. Perhaps there's been a change in the rotation I wasn't informed about.'

He stepped out into the hallway, leaving the door slightly ajar. Mary could hear muffled voices, the doctor's tone becoming increasingly concerned as he spoke to someone. She strained to hear, catching fragments of the conversation.

'...blonde nurse? Are you sure?'

'...not on our staff...'

'...check the security footage...'

The voices faded as they moved further down the hallway. Mary looked at Ted, her eyes wide with growing apprehension. 'Ted, something's not right. Why wouldn't they know about a nurse taking our baby?'

Ted tried to smile reassuringly, but it didn't quite reach his eyes. 'I'm sure it's just a miscommunication. You know how hectic hospitals can be.' Despite his words, he stood up and began pacing the small room, his movements jerky and tense.

Minutes ticked by, feeling like hours. The beeping of machines in the room seemed to grow louder, more insistent. Mary found herself counting the seconds between each beep, anything to distract herself from the gnawing worry in her gut.

Finally, the doctor returned, accompanied by a nurse and a man in a security uniform. The doctor's face was pale, his earlier friendly demeanour replaced by barely concealed concern.

'Mr. and Mrs. Brown,' he began, his voice carefully

controlled, 'can you describe the nurse who took your daughter? Any details you can remember would be helpful.'

Mary's heart began to race, her arms tightening instinctively around her son. 'She was blonde, medium height. She seemed friendly and confident. She was wearing a standard nurse's uniform, I think. Why? What's happening?'

The security guard stepped forward, his face grim. 'Ma'am, we've checked the logs and security footage. There's no record of any nurse entering your room in the last hour, and none of our staff match that description.'

A chill ran down Mary's spine, her voice rising in pitch as panic began to set in. 'No, that's not possible. A nurse was just here. She had blonde hair, she was wearing a uniform. She said it would only take a few minutes for the check-up.'

The doctor turned to Ted, his voice low and urgent. 'Mr. Brown, how long ago did this nurse take your daughter?'

Ted glanced at his watch, his hands visibly shaking. 'Maybe... ten minutes ago? Fifteen at most.' His voice cracked as he asked, 'What's going on?'

The doctor took a deep breath, clearly trying to maintain his professional composure. 'I'm going to alert hospital security and contact the police immediately. There may be a mistake, but we must act quickly to ensure your daughter's safety.'

As the reality of the situation began to sink in, Mary felt as if the air had been sucked out of the room. The steady beeping of the heart monitor seemed to echo the frantic pounding in her chest. She looked down at her son, peacefully sleeping in her arms, unaware of the storm brewing around him. Then her gaze shifted to the empty space beside her, where her daughter should have been.

In that moment, the world seemed to tilt on its axis. What had begun as a day of joy and new beginnings had rapidly descended into a nightmare. As the room erupted into a flurry of activity, with staff rushing in and out and voices raised in urgent discussion, Mary and Ted clung to each other and their son, united in their fear and desperate hope that their daughter would be safely returned to them.

Ted moved to sit beside Mary on the bed, wrapping an arm around her shoulders. 'I'm sure it's fine. Like the doctor said, probably just a mix-up. She'll be back any minute now.'

But as the minutes ticked by, the knot in Mary's stomach grew. She could feel panic rising in her chest, threatening to overwhelm her. 'Ted, something's wrong. I can feel it. We need to find her. Now.'

Ted nodded, his own fear evident in his tight jaw and clenched fists. He stood up, pacing the small room. 'I'll go look for her. She can't have gone far.'

Just as Ted reached for the door handle, the doctor returned, his face grave. 'Mr. and Mrs. Brown, I'm afraid we have a situation. We've checked with all the nursing staff, and no one was authorised to take your daughter for any tests.'

Mary felt the blood drain from her face. The room seemed to spin around her. 'What are you saying?' she whispered, her voice barely audible.

A sudden, piercing alarm drowned out the doctor's next words. The hospital's security system had been activated.

Alarms blared as the hospital went into lockdown. Security guards appeared as if by magic, their faces grim. Nurses and doctors rushed about, checking every room, every closet.

In the chaos that erupted, Mary clung to her son, her eyes wild with fear and disbelief. Ted stood frozen, his face a mask of shock and dawning horror.

'Our daughter,' Mary whispered, her voice breaking. 'Someone took our baby girl.'

The investigation unfolded with methodical cruelty. Each detail emerged like a piece of a terrible puzzle: no nurse matching the description on duty, no scheduled check-ups, no record in the system.

The police arrived, asking questions that Mary and Ted could barely process. What did the nurse look like? What was she wearing? Did they notice anything unusual?

All Mary could remember was a kind smile, a cool, gentle touch. She had blonde hair. What else was there? How could they have known they needed to look closely? How could they have suspected anything?

As Police reviewed the security footage, a grainy image appeared on the screen: a woman in a nurse's uniform carrying a small bundle. She moved with purpose, nodding to other staff as she passed. No one stopped her, and no one questioned her.

The image of the woman exiting the hospital, their baby girl in her arms, would be burned into Mary and Ted's retinas forever.

A police woman arrived within minutes and introduced herself as Detective Inspector Matthews, her quiet competence a stark contrast to the emotional maelstrom surrounding her. She studied the security footage with forensic attention, noting the imposter's confident stride, the way other staff yielded to her assumed authority.

'She knew the hospital's routines,' the police officer observed. 'This wasn't opportunistic.'

'The man in the restaurant,' Mary suddenly recalled, her voice hoarse. 'The one who watched us. He was here, in the corridor. I saw him.'

Detective Matthews' attention sharpened. 'Tell me everything about this man.'

As the investigation gathered momentum, patterns emerged. The mysterious observer, the precisely timed appearance of the false nurse, the too-perfect execution of the abduction—all suggested an orchestration beyond simple opportunity.

As the reality of the situation crashed over them like a tidal wave, Mary felt a scream building in her throat. It started as a low moan, growing in volume and intensity until it echoed through the hospital corridors, a sound of pure anguish that seemed to shake the very foundations of the building.

'She's stolen my baby,' Mary sobbed, clutching her son even tighter. 'She's stolen our little girl.'

Mary felt like a chasm had opened within her, swallowing every ounce of joy and hope she'd ever known.

Her legs gave way beneath her, and she crumpled to the cold hospital floor. The pain that ripped through her chest was physical as if someone had reached inside and torn out her still-beating heart.

'No,' she whispered, the word a desperate prayer. 'No, no, no.'

Ted held her and their son close, both of them shaking with shock and grief; they knew that their lives had changed irrevocably. The joy of becoming parents, the humour of their pregnancy misadventures, the excitement of starting a new chapter - this unthinkable tragedy overshadowed all of it.

Mary's arms ached with emptiness, yearning for the weight of her baby girl. She could still feel the phantom warmth of her daughter's tiny body and smell the sweet scent of her newborn skin. How could she be gone? How could Mary have let this happen?

She should have known. She should have protected her child. What kind of mother was she to let a stranger walk away with her baby? The thought sent a fresh surge of agony through her, and this time, the scream tore free from her throat, echoing off the sterile hospital walls.

Ted was there, his arms around her, his voice in her ear, but she couldn't make out the words. All she could hear was the deafening silence where her daughter's cries should be. All she could feel was the gaping void in her chest, a black hole of grief threatening to consume her entirely.

Images flashed through her mind in cruel succession: her daughter's first smile, never to be seen; first steps, never to be taken; first words, never to be heard. A lifetime of moments, stolen in an instant.

The horror of it all threatened to unhinge her. Where was her baby now? Was she scared? Hungry? Crying for a mother who wasn't there to comfort her? The thought sent Mary spiralling further into despair.

She clutched at Ted, her fingers digging into his arms, anchoring herself to him as the storm of grief raged within her. 'We have to find her,' she choked out between sobs. 'We have to... I can't... I can't breathe without her.'

The world around her blurred, faces and voices melding into a cacophony of meaningless noise. Nothing mattered except the absence of her child. The emptiness inside her yawned wider, threatening to swallow her whole.

A part of her had been ripped away, leaving a wound so deep and raw that she wasn't sure it could ever heal. The only thing that could fill this void was her daughter, safe in her arms once more.

FRANTIC SEARCH BEGINS

The maternity ward of Kingston Hospital, usually a place of joy and new beginnings, had transformed into a scene of controlled chaos. Police officers moved purposefully through the halls, their urgent whispers and radio communications creating a tense atmosphere that pulsed with the frantic energy of the search.

In the centre of this storm, Mary and Ted Brown sat shell-shocked on the edge of the hospital bed, their son cradled protectively between them. They looked like survivors of some great tragedy, their eyes wide and unfocused, their responses to questions mechanical and distant.

Detective Sarah Bronson, a no-nonsense woman with a stern demeanour, stood before them, notepad in hand. 'Mr. and Mrs. Brown, I need you to focus. Can you describe the nurse again?'

Mary blinked slowly, as if emerging from a deep fog. 'She was... friendly. She smiled. I remember thinking how kind she seemed.' Her voice broke as the reality of the situation hit her anew. 'How could we have been so wrong?'

Ted, his face pale with worry, attempted to help. 'She had

blonde hair, I think. Medium height. She was wearing the standard nurse uniform. It all happened so fast.'

Detective Bronson nodded, her expression softening slightly. 'Every detail helps. we are doing everything we can to find your daughter. Do you remember whether her hands were warm or cold?'

'Cold. They were cold,' said Mary, the memory of the cool touch coming back to her. 'Why does it matter?'

'Well, if she had cold hands, it's likely that she came from outside. We'll scan CCTV to see who left, but we can also check to see who arrived recently.'

A team of technicians hunched over monitors in the hospital's security office, reviewing footage with intense concentration. Officer Jenkins, a young rookie, called out to his superior. 'Sir, I think I've got something.'

The security chief leaned in, scrutinising the grainy image of a woman arriving at the hospital. It was the same woman they'd seen leaving with a baby, but this image showed her face more clearly.

'Good work, Jenkins. Get this to Detective Bronson immediately.'

The afternoon sun beat down mercilessly on the hospital car park, now a sea of gleaming news vans and restless reporters. The air buzzed with tension and the low hum of equipment, punctuated by the occasional shout of a cameraman or the sharp click of a photographer's shutter.

Among the throng stood Jake Morrison, a wiry man with a shock of prematurely grey hair and eyes that constantly darted, missing nothing. His rumpled suit and loosened tie spoke of long hours on the job, but the glint in his eye betrayed an unwavering determination. This story could make his career, and he wasn't about to let hospital security stand in his way.

Jake's gaze swept the building's facade, noting the positions of guards and staff. His fingers drummed an impatient rhythm on his notepad as he waited, biding his time. Then, like a cat sensing an open door, he saw his opportunity.

A delivery van pulled up to the service entrance, momentarily distracting the security guard. In that split second, Jake moved. He slipped through the door, his movements fluid and practised. Once inside, he straightened his tie and adopted the hurried walk of a man with purpose, blending seamlessly into the organised chaos of the hospital corridors.

The maternity ward was quiet, the air heavy with a mix of disinfectant and lingering fear. Jake's steps slowed as he approached room 302, his ears straining for any sound of movement. Hearing nothing, he gently pushed the door open.

Mary Brown sat alone by the window, a solitary figure bathed in the warm glow of the setting sun. Her shoulders were slumped, her gaze fixed on some distant point beyond the glass. The empty cot beside her bed seemed to cry out in accusation of its missing occupant. In the other cot lay a tiny, sleeping baby. That must be George, he thought

Jake cleared his throat softly, adopting a gentle demeanour. 'Mrs. Brown?' he said, his voice barely above a whisper. 'I'm Jake Morrison. I can't imagine what you're going through right now.'

Mary turned, her movements slow and pained. Her eyes, red-rimmed and sunken, met Jake's. For a moment, neither spoke.

'I know you've been through hell,' Jake continued, taking a cautious step forward. 'But your story... it could help. It could be the key to finding your daughter. People need to hear it to understand. To help.'

Mary's lips trembled, her voice cracking as she spoke. 'We just want her back. Our little girl...' Her words trailed off, choked by a sob.

Jake leaned in, his recorder discreetly capturing every word. 'Tell me about her. Help us understand what's been taken from you.'

Just as Mary opened her mouth to respond, the door burst open. A nurse rushed in, her face flushed with anger and exertion. 'You can't be in here!' she exclaimed, moving swiftly to place herself between Jake and Mary.

Jake backed away, hands raised in a gesture of surrender, but his eyes never left Mary. As the nurse ushered him out, Mary's quiet sobs echoed in his ears, a haunting soundtrack to the story he was already composing in his mind.

DETECTIVE INSPECTOR SARAH BRONSON commanded the makeshift incident room with quiet authority. Her carefully neutral expression betrayed nothing of the urgency she felt, though her eyes held the sharp focus of a predator tracking its quarry. Twenty years of service had taught her that the first hours of a child abduction were crucial.

Officers were hunched over computers, following every possible lead.

'Johnson,' Bronson called out, 'what have we got on the security footage?'

Johnson, a tech specialist, pulled up an image on the main screen. 'We've isolated a few frames where we can see the suspect's face. It's not great quality, but-'

'OK, that's a decent image. Can we get everything we can, and I'll take them through to the room at the end of the corridor? Can someone get Mary and Ted and take them through?'

THE HARSH FLUORESCENT lights of the small consulting room cast an unforgiving glare over its occupants. Mary sat rigid in her chair, her fingers intertwined so tightly that her knuckles had turned white. The air felt thick and heavy with tension and the lingering scent of stale coffee. Across the table, Detective Bronson's piercing gaze never wavered as she slid a glossy photograph across the polished surface.

'Mrs Brown,' Bronson began, her tone calibrated to convey both authority and empathy, 'I need you to focus on the details. Even the smallest observation could be significant.'

Mary sat with unnatural stillness, one hand clasped in Ted's, the other resting protectively over George's sleeping form. Her voice emerged as though from a great distance. 'She seemed... practiced. Confident. The sort of presence you'd expect in a medical professional.'

'That's...' Mary's voice faltered, her brow furrowing in concentration. 'That's not the woman who collected the baby from me.' She looked up, meeting Bronson's steady gaze. 'But she does look familiar. I think... I think she might be the nurse who saw me when I came in for the scan.'

Beside her, Ted leaned forward, his presence a comforting warmth against her arm. His face was drawn, dark circles under his eyes betraying sleepless nights and endless worry. 'Are you sure, love?' he asked softly, his voice rough with emotion.

Mary nodded, her certainty growing. 'Yes, I'm sure. I remember her blonde hair, and...' She paused, a fragment of memory surfacing. 'She had a name badge. It said 'Joy' on it.'

Ted's eyes widened in recognition. 'That's right! And it had a smiley face after it. I remember thinking it was a bit odd for a hospital.'

Detective Bronson and her partner exchanged a significant look. 'A smiley face?' Bronson repeated, her tone carefully neutral. 'She wanted to appear friendly, approachable. Someone you'd trust with your child.'

. . .

The implications of this statement hung in the air, adding another layer to the already oppressive atmosphere. Mary felt a chill run down her spine, her mind racing to process this new information.

Bronson cleared her throat, breaking the tense silence. 'We have some CCTV footage I'd like you to look at as well, Mrs Brown. Are you ready?'

Mary nodded, steeling herself. Bronson opened her ipad, and set it up so Mary could see the screen. The footage was grainy, but clear enough to make out a figure walking purposefully down a hospital corridor, a small bundle cradled in her arms.

Mary's heart leapt into her throat. 'That's her!' she exclaimed, her voice rising with fear and relief. 'That's the woman who came to our room. I'm sure of it. What do you think, Ted?'

She felt Ted's hand close over hers, his grip tightening. The detectives leaned forward, their interest palpable.

'It could have been. I'm not sure, to be honest. I didn't really notice her.'

'So, are there two women involved in this? What's going on?'

Bronson glanced at her assistant. 'We think so. Now let me show you something else.'

Another photo appeared on the screen, showing a man standing outside the hospital. He was partially turned away from the camera, but his profile was visible.

Mary's breath caught. A memory stirred, hazy but insistent. 'That's him. It's the man from the restaurant. It's the man who I keep seeing everywhere.

'I've met him before. I know I have. Christ, who is that?'

SHE'S STOLEN MY BABY

Her frustration mounted as she struggled to place the familiar face.

'I wish I could remember where I know him from. He's definitely, definitely been following me though. I keep seeing him everywhere.

'He was sitting at the restaurant the night we told our mums I was pregnant. He kept looking over at us. I remember thinking it was odd, but...' She trailed off, the implications of this connection beginning to sink in.

Detective Bronson's partner, a stocky man with kind eyes, spoke up for the first time. 'This is excellent, Mr and Mrs Brown. You've given us some very valuable information.'

Mary turned to them, her eyes bright with unshed tears and a desperate hope. 'Do you think this means you're close to finding her? Our baby?'

Bronson's face softened, a hint of compassion breaking through her professional demeanour. 'we are following every lead, Mrs Brown. This information will certainly help narrow our search.'

As the detectives conferred in low voices, Mary leaned into Ted's embrace, drawing strength from his steady presence. The room around them faded away as she closed her eyes, conjuring an image of her daughter's face.

'we are going to find her, love,' Ted murmured, his lips brushing against her hair. 'we are going to bring her home.'

Mary nodded, unable to speak past the lump in her throat. Outside the window, the sun was setting. As darkness fell, Mary clung to a glimmer of hope, fragile but persistent. Somewhere out there, their daughter was waiting to be found.

'What do you think all this means, detective? Please be honest with me.'

'This kidnapping was probably premeditated.'

The revelation of premeditation struck Mary with physical force. The room seemed to tilt on its axis as the full implications crystallised in her mind. The edges of her vision darkened, her body's response to overwhelming stress manifesting in a sudden loss of consciousness.

Ted caught her just before she hit the floor, cradling her in his arms as medical staff rushed to assist. 'Mary? Mary, honey, can you hear me?'

As nurses tended to Mary and Detective Bronson barked orders into her radio; Ted held his wife close, his voice a hoarse whisper. 'Hold on, Mary. we are going to find her. we are going to bring our daughter home.'

THE INVESTIGATION DEEPENS

The rhythmic click of heels against hospital linoleum announced the arrival of reinforcements. Rosie appeared first, her usual poise replaced by barely contained anguish. The perfectly styled hair and immaculate clothing that typically defined her seemed suddenly irrelevant in the face of family crisis.

Rosie's eyes, red-rimmed and wild, darted around the room before settling on her daughter.

'Mary, my darling,' she breathed, gathering her daughter into an embrace that spoke volumes beyond words. Mary yielded to her mother's arms, allowing herself to be held as she hadn't since childhood. The facade of strength she'd maintained crumbled momentarily, replaced by raw need for maternal comfort.

Ted stood nearby, his own eyes glistening with unshed tears as he watched the reunion. He placed a gentle hand on Rosie's back, offering what little comfort he could.

Rosie pulled back, cupping Mary's face in her hands. 'we are going to find her, do you hear me? I don't care what it takes. I'll tear this city apart brick by brick if I have to.'

Detective Inspector Bronson observed the scene with professional distance, though her eyes registered every detail of the family dynamics unfolding before her. These interactions often revealed subtle clues that could prove crucial to an investigation.

They had been trying to assemble all the facts they could about Mary's pregnancy and everything that had happened since the birth.

Mary's recollection emerged in fragments: the mysterious man at the restaurant, his companion with her too-intense gaze, the nurse who wouldn't meet their eyes, the inexplicable arrival of the silver rattle.

Rosie saw Bronson watching them. 'You,' she said, her voice low and dangerous. 'Why aren't you out there looking for my granddaughter? And why in God's name are there vultures with cameras camped outside? They're harassing everyone who comes in or out!'

To her credit, Detective Bronson didn't flinch under Rosie's intense scrutiny. 'I assure you we are doing everything in our power to locate your granddaughter. As for the press, they can be quite helpful in getting the word out.'

'Helpful?' Rosie's voice rose an octave. 'They're not helpful, they're intrusive! They're turning my family's pain into entertainment!'

As Rosie continued her tirade, the door opened once more. Edna, Ted's mother, slipped in quietly, her face a mask of worry and exhaustion. Ted immediately went to her, wrapping her in a tight hug.

'Oh, Teddy,' Edna whispered, her voice cracking. 'I came as soon as I could. Have they... is there any news?'

Ted shook his head, unable to form words. Edna's face crumpled, and she clutched her son tighter.

Rosie, momentarily distracted from her argument with Detective Bronson, turned to see Edna. The two women stared at each other for a split second, years of rivalry and petty disagreements flashing between them. Then, as if a switch had been flipped, they moved as one, coming together in a fierce embrace.

'Oh, Edna,' Rosie sobbed, her anger giving way to raw grief.

'I know, I know,' Edna murmured, her tears falling freely.

Mary and Ted watched in stunned silence as their mothers, who had once bickered over who would be the favourite grandmother, now clung to each other, united in their shared pain and fear.

Detective Bronson spoke softly, perhaps sensing a moment to smooth things over. 'Mrs Brown,' Bronson began, her tone measured, 'we need to establish a complete timeline of the pregnancy. Every appointment, every interaction, no matter how insignificant it might seem. We're busy following up everything Mary and Ted tell us - we are doing everything we can.'

In an instant, both women's heads snapped up, their tear-streaked faces morphing into identical expressions of indignation. 'Doing everything you can? W'hat - standing here, drinking hospital coffee and watching us? Is that really the best you can do?'

Detective Bronson was visibly taken aback by the sudden shift. Despite the gravity of the situation, Mary felt a small bubble of warmth in her chest. Here were her mother and mother-in-law, setting aside their differences and presenting a united front in the face of this crisis.

As Rosie and Edna continued to berate the detective, their voices overlapping in a duet of maternal fury, Mary leaned into Ted's side. He wrapped an arm around her, pulling her close. Her hand lay on George, sleeping in his cot next to them.

Bronson slipped out of the room.

BERNICE BLOOM

In another wing of the hospital, Officer Jenkins conducted staff interviews with methodical precision. The suspect's photo elicited no recognition—a telling detail in itself. In a department where staff routinely crossed paths, a complete absence of recognition suggested something more sinister than opportunistic theft.

'She infiltrated the hospital with professional expertise,' Bronson noted to her team. 'The uniform, the terminology, the confidence to move through restricted areas—this suggests extensive planning and resources.'

'Or a knowledge of hospitals and how they operate?' suggested a young officer. 'I mean - someone who used to work here? Or someone who works here, but in a different department?'

'Does Mary know anyone who works here?' asked Jenkins.

'I'll find out.'

Bronson walked back into the room, and approached Mary and Ted.

'We need another quick word with you,' she said. 'Perhaps you could join me?'

Mary eased herself out of the chair. Ted lifted George out of his cot and carried him through to the control room. They sat down at the table indicated by Bronson.

The detective's face was a mask of professional detachment, but the dark circles under her eyes betrayed the incredible amount of stress she was under.

'Mr. and Mrs. Brown,' she began, her voice gravelly from fatigue. 'Do you know anyone who works at this, or any other hospital?'

'No. You've asked us this before,' said Ted.

'Not just nursing staff or doctors, but anyone at all who has worked in a hospital - as a porter, in catering or in security.'

SHE'S STOLEN MY BABY

Mary and Ted looked at one another and shrugged before Ted confirmed to the officer that they didn't know anyone.

'OK. Look, I need you to walk me through every detail of your pregnancy and delivery. Leave nothing out, no matter how insignificant it might seem.'

Ted cleared his throat and began recounting their experiences, from the early days of the pregnancy to the delivery. They described routine check-ups, birthing classes, and their interactions with hospital staff.

Detective Bronson listened intently as they spoke, her pen moving swiftly across her notepad. 'Did you notice anyone paying unusual attention to you during your hospital visits? Any strangers who seemed overly interested in your pregnancy?'

Mary furrowed her brow, thinking hard. She'd already told the officer about the man in the restaurant and the woman sitting next to him. She'd mentioned the nurse with the wild curly hair who refused to make eye contact with them on their visit to the hospital for the scan and they'd mentioned the rattle that was sent to the house. Was there anything else to say? She tried to fill in the gaps, with details about everything they had done, however banal it seemed.

The detective listened, interrupted with more questions and tried her hardest to understand what was happening.

'Have you made any enemies? Does anyone wish you harm? Do you have friends who want a baby?' The questions came thick and fast.

'Do you have a ring doorbell?'
'No.'
'Do your neighbours have ring doorbells?'
'Some of them do, yes.'

. . .

MEANWHILE, in another part of the hospital, Officer Jenkins was questioning the staff, showing them security camera photos of the suspect.

'I'm sorry,' a tired-looking nurse said, squinting at the image. 'After a 12-hour shift, faces start to blur together. I can't say for certain if I've seen her.'

No one recognised the mystery woman who had taken Mary's baby.

'She's not a nurse. She can't be,' Detective Bronson said to her team. 'She's not on any hospital records, and as far as we can see, she's not among the agency nurses on staff. Someone in the hospital would have recognised her. Also, Mary recalls the woman's hands being cold. I think she'd come in from outside, either wearing a uniform she'd acquired previously or stealing a uniform from the hospital. The question is - why has she done this? Why Mary? And who is the guy Mary said was staring at her in the restaurant?'

Back with the Browns, a sketch artist worked diligently to capture the likeness of the suspicious nurse and the man and woman from the restaurant. It was a painstaking process, with Mary and Ted straining to recall every detail.

THE PHYSICAL REMINDERS of motherhood proved particularly cruel. Mary's body continued its biological imperative, producing milk for a baby she couldn't nurture. Each expression of milk became both necessity and torment, filling bottles that stood as stark reminders of absence.

Ted found Mary in their hospital room, tears streaming down her face as she used a breast pump to bottle all the leftover milk after feeding her son.

'Oh, honey,' Ted said softly, his heart breaking at the sight.

Mary looked up, her eyes red and puffy. 'What if she's hungry? What if they're not feeding her properly?'

. . .

AS EVENING APPROACHED, Mary and Ted faced another challenge: a press conference. Detective Bronson gave them a final briefing, emphasising the importance of appealing to the kidnapper's humanity.

Standing before a sea of cameras and microphones, Mary and Ted made their plea. Mary's voice shook as she spoke. 'To the person who took our daughter... please, bring her back to us. She needs her mum and dad.'

Ted, his hand firmly grasping Mary's, added, 'We just want our little girl back. No questions asked.'

As they finished their statement, Detective Bronson fielded questions, deflecting the more sensational inquiries and focusing on the facts of the case.

Exhausted and emotionally drained, Mary and Ted retreated to their room. As they settled back into the now-familiar routine of waiting and worrying, neither could have predicted the breakthrough that was about to come.

MILES FROM THE HOSPITAL, in a modest flat in Croydon, Sandra Mitchell sat before her television, recognition dawning as she watched the press conference. The woman she'd seen—glimpsed really—walking with purpose through her neighbourhood suddenly took on new significance.

With shaking hands, she reached for her phone and dialled the tip line. 'Hello?' she said, her voice barely above a whisper. 'I... I think I might know something about the missing baby.'

Detective Bronson received the tip with cautious optimism. Experience had taught her that hope required careful management, both for the investigating team and the victims' family. She ordered immediate surveillance of the Croydon location while maintaining absolute secrecy.

She couldn't tell Mary and Ted. This might lead to nothing, and the last thing she wanted was to raise their hopes. Deep within her, though, she hoped this could be the break they'd been praying for.

As night settled over London, multiple scenarios played out simultaneously. In Croydon, surveillance teams took up positions with practiced stealth. In the hospital, two grandmothers maintained their protective watch. And somewhere between these points, a woman with blonde hair sang a lullaby to a baby who didn't belong to her, while a man stood beside her, more terrified than he'd ever been in his life.

Detective Bronson stood at her incident room window, studying the city lights. Years of experience told her they were close—perhaps closer than they'd been since this began. But experience had also taught her that these moments were often the most dangerous.

FALSE HOPES AND DEAD ENDS

☙

The pre-dawn light cast long shadows across the Croydon estate as Detective Inspector Bronson briefed her tactical team. The building before them stood unremarkable among its neighbours—a perfect hiding place for those who wished to remain invisible.

'Alpha Team, take point,' Bronson instructed, her voice pitched low. 'Remember, we are potentially dealing with a newborn. Proceed with extreme caution.'

The armed response unit moved with practised efficiency, their training evident in every controlled movement. Officer Jenkins led the ascent, each step calculated to minimise noise. Bronson stood to the side. She would be the voice in the operation.

The corridor stretched before them, identical doors lining both sides. The suspect's flat—number 47—waited at the end, its peeling paint and brass numerals offering no hint of what lay behind.

'Police! Open your door!' Bronson's command echoed through the hallway.

Silence.

With a nod, the battering ram came out. The door gave way with a splintering crash, and the team poured into the apartment, shouting commands to an empty room.

As the dust settled, it became clear that their quarry had flown the coop. The apartment bore all the hallmarks of a hasty departure - drawers left open, clothes strewn about, and a half-eaten sandwich on the counter.

'Spread out,' Bronson ordered. 'Search every inch. I want to know what this woman had for breakfast three Tuesdays ago.'

As the team combed through the apartment, Jenkins made his way to the bedroom, his face scrunched in concentration. He was determined to find that crucial piece of evidence that would crack the case wide open.

And then he saw it. A small pile of fabric peeking out from under the bed. With trembling hands, he reached out and pulled...

'Detective.' he cried, his voice cracking with excitement. 'I found baby clothes.'

Bronson was by his side in an instant, her eyes widening at the sight. There, clutched in Jenkins's hands like the Holy Grail, was a onesie. And not just any onesie - this one proudly proclaimed 'I JUST DID 9 MONTHS ON THE INSIDE' in garish neon letters.

'Good work, Jenkins,' Bronson said, her voice uncharacteristically soft. 'Bag it for evidence.'

Jenkins placed the onesie in an evidence bag as if it were made of spun glass instead of slightly stained cotton.

As the search continued, more items were uncovered—formula, nappies, and baby cream. Each discovery sent a ripple of excitement through the team. This had to be it. They were close. They could feel it.

Back at the hospital, Mary's strength wavered under the weight of continued uncertainty. She cradled George close, his presence both comfort and reminder of what was missing.

'Who would do this?' she whispered, her voice raw. 'What kind of person steals a baby from her mother?

'I don't know how I'll cope if they don't find her. I won't be able to live. I just know it. Who would do this to us, Ted?'

She held her little boy close as she rocked him gently while her mind whirred with terrifying scenarios. 'I'm worried I'll never see her again? What if they harm her? Ted, what are we going to do?'

'Sssshhhh…' he said, rocking her gently in his arms. 'Try not think like that. She'll be back with us soon.'

'I WANT to go out for some fresh air, said Mary. 'I need to get some fresh air into my lungs before I collapse.'

'I don't think that's wise,' said the detective. 'There are a lot of people out there. Journalists everywhere.'

'I don't care. I can't be cooped up here any more. I just want to walk a few steps outside.'

'OK,' said the detective. 'I'll gather some officers to go with you.'

As they made their way along the corridor to the lift and down to the main reception area, Mary saw the large crowd of reporters outside. But it wasn't until she walked out that they realised the media frenzy had reached new heights.

The hospital exit became an inadvertent press conference. Cameras tracked their movement like predatory beings, each lens hoping to capture the perfect moment of parental anguish. Mary faced them with unexpected composure.

'If anyone has information about our daughter, come forward. She needs to be home with her family.'

Once journalists realised she was talking, microphones

were thrust in her face before she could fully exit the building, despite the efforts of the police to keep people back. Questions were shouted from all directions, creating a cacophony of noise that made Mary want to bury her head in her hands.

'Mr. and Mrs. Brown. Is it true you've found your daughter?'

'Were there signs of foul play?'

'Ted. Ted. Can you tell us how you're feeling?'

As they pushed their way through the crowd, Mary leaned in close to Ted. 'I swear, if one more person asks me how I'm feeling, I'm going to show them exactly how I'm feeling. With my fists.'

Ted nodded sympathetically. 'I know, honey. Just remember that the more they write about our missing baby, the more people will be looking out for her.'

'That's a good point,' said Mary, turning to face the bank of cameras.

'Thank you for all your help,' she said. 'I'm so desperate to have my daughter back that I can hardly breathe. Thank you for helping me. Please - if anyone knows anything - go to the police straight away. I beg you.'

Ted helped his crying wife back inside while the photographers pushed up towards them, eager to get a close-up photograph of the crying mother.

Back in the police station, the investigation continued at a feverish pace and would do so through the night. Detective Bronson, running on nothing but coffee and sheer determination, followed every lead, no matter how tenuous.

A reported sighting of a suspicious van led to an hour-long stakeout, only for it to be revealed as a plumber's vehicle.

Another promising lead turned out to be a tourist with an unhealthy obsession with lifelike dolls. The woman, clutching two disturbingly realistic baby dolls, seemed more offended by the implication that her 'children' weren't real than by the accusation of kidnapping.

THE FOLLOWING MORNING, Mary and Ted were told they could return home. Mary was torn; she wanted to be back in familiar surroundings, but loathed the idea of being away from the hospital; the last place she saw her daughter.

Their return home introduced new forms of torment. Phantom cries echoed through the house, sending her rushing to the nursery multiple times a day, even though their son slept in the bed with them. The nursery was empty.

But nothing could convince Mary.

Ted found her there one night, cradling a pillow and singing a soft lullaby. The sight broke his heart all over again.

'Mary,' he said gently, kneeling beside her. 'Honey, come back to bed.'

Mary looked up at him, her eyes glazed and unfocused. 'I heard her crying, Ted. She needs me.'

Ted swallowed hard, fighting back his tears. 'I know, sweetheart. But she's not here. Not yet. But we'll find her, I promise.'

While the Browns grappled with their private hell, other scenes played out across London. In a basement office, intelligence analysts traced international phone calls. In suburban streets, police patrols maintained their vigilance. And somewhere, behind an anonymous door, a woman prepared a bottle with practiced care, while a man dropped to the floor, crawled into the foetus position and cried.

CCTV

The next morning, Ted gazed at Mary, curled up on the sofa in her faded pink flannel pyjamas, her eyes vacant and red-rimmed. The morning sunlight filtering through the curtains cast a soft glow on her unwashed hair. He tugged his navy towelling dressing gown tighter, steeling himself with determination.

'I'm getting us the best breakfast ever,' he said, forcing cheer into his voice. 'Today, we will dine like kings.'

He grabbed his phone and placed a huge breakfast order on Deliveroo. Mary wasn't eating properly - this might tempt her into eating something.

Thirty minutes later, the doorbell chimed. Ted hurried to answer, the plush carpet muffling his bare footsteps. A bemused delivery driver stood on their doorstep, arms straining with bags that wafted tantalising aromas of bacon and coffee.

Ted ferried the feast to their kitchen, unpacking container after container onto the granite countertop. The rich scent of a full English breakfast filled the air - smoky bacon, savoury sausages, earthy mushrooms, and the sharp tang of grilled tomatoes.

'Look, honey,' Ted called softly, arranging plates on a tray. 'We've got everything here. Crispy bacon, sausages, eggs done three ways, grilled tomatoes, mushrooms, baked beans, hash browns, and even black pudding. Oh, and don't forget the toast - white and brown.'

He carried the loaded tray to the living room, where Mary sat motionless, staring out the window. The curtains fluttered in a gentle breeze, carrying the scent of their neighbour's blooming roses.

Ted set the tray on the coffee table. He picked up a piece of golden-brown toast, the butter melting into its crisp surface. 'Come on, love. Just a little bite? You need to keep your strength up.'

Mary's gaze flickered to the food, then away. She pulled her knees closer to her chest, her pink pyjamas wrinkling. 'I'm not hungry, Ted. I can't... I just can't.'

Ted's heart sank. He set the toast down and sank onto the sofa beside her, the leather creaking under his weight. He wrapped an arm around her shoulders, feeling how fragile she'd become. 'I know it's hard, but you have to eat something. For your health, for... for when she comes back.'

At the mention of their missing daughter, Mary's breath hitched. She buried her face in her hands, her shoulders shaking with silent sobs. The room filled with the ticking of the clock and the muffled sounds of her grief.

Ted felt helpless, the steaming breakfast now seeming like a cruel joke. He rubbed soothing circles on Mary's back, the soft flannel warm under his palm. 'I'm sorry, love. I just... I don't know what to do. Tell me how to help you.'

After a long moment, Mary lifted her head. Her eyes, once bright and full of life, were now red-rimmed and puffy. She reached out with a trembling hand and picked up a piece of toast. Ted held his breath as she took a small bite, chewing mechanically.

'There you go,' he encouraged softly. 'That's my girl.'

Mary managed two more bites before her face suddenly paled, the toast falling from her fingers onto the plush rug. She clapped a hand over her mouth and bolted for the downstairs bathroom, her bare feet slapping against the hardwood floor.

Ted followed, the sounds of retching echoing off the bathroom tiles. He knelt beside her on the cold floor, holding back her tangled hair and murmuring soothing words as she emptied what little was in her stomach.

When the heaving finally subsided, Mary slumped against him, exhausted. The harsh bathroom light emphasised the dark circles under her eyes. 'I'm sorry,' she whispered, her voice raw. 'I wanted to eat, I really did. But all I can think about is her. Is she hungry? Is someone feeding her? Does she miss us?'

Ted gathered her into his arms, the terrycloth of his robe absorbing her tears. He pressed a kiss to her forehead, breathing in the faint scent of her shampoo. 'It's okay, love. You have nothing to be sorry for. we are going to get through this together, I promise.'

As he held his wife on the cold bathroom floor, the house filled with the now-cooling breakfast and the lingering scent of sickness, Ted had never felt more powerless.

'Is there anything I can do to help?' asked Ted.

'Yes - I want to go back to the hospital. I want to be where we last saw her.'

'OK,' said Ted. 'Come on. Let's go back there.'

THE HOSPITAL CORRIDORS seemed different now—no longer

simply institutional spaces but a maze of memories, each turn reminding them of their last moments with Daisy.

The stark white painted walls and the persistent scent of disinfectant. It was as if she'd never left.

Mary's footsteps echoed hollowly as she walked beside Ted, her hand nestled in his. She felt the oppressive weight of the place, but she was still pleased to be there…she needed to be back where she'd last held Daisy.

'Do you fancy a coffee?' he asked as they walked past the Costa Coffee in the corner of the hospital's main entrance.

Mary nodded, managing a wan smile that didn't quite reach her eyes. Ted couldn't help but notice how pale she looked under the harsh fluorescent light.

The coffee shop was a bustling oasis of normalcy in the hospital's clinical environment. The rich aroma of freshly ground coffee beans permeated the air, mingling with the sweet scent of pastries. The warm lighting and soft background music created an atmosphere that was a stark contrast to the tension-filled hospital rooms all around them.

'Why don't you find us a seat, love?' Ted suggested, gently guiding Mary towards a quiet corner. 'I'll get us some coffee.'

Ted joined the queue and looked around at the other patrons. A young couple cradling a newborn, their faces a mixture of exhaustion and pure joy. An elderly man sipping tea, his gnarled hands wrapped around the warm mug. A harried-looking doctor gulping down what was probably her fifth coffee of the day. Each person carried their own story, their reasons for being here in this place of beginnings and endings.

When he reached the counter, Ted was greeted by a cheerful barista with a shock of bright blue hair. 'What can I get for you today?' she chirped, her smile seemingly at odds with the sombre hospital setting.

As Ted placed his order, his gaze drifted to the barista's

name badge. Suddenly, the world around him seemed to screech to a halt. There, pinned to her apron, was a badge that read 'Zoe' followed by a smiley face.

He looked at the other baristas. Those he could see had the same marking on their badges: their name followed by a smiley face.

Ted's heart began to race, his palms growing clammy as the implications of this discovery crashed over him. He mumbled something about forgetting his wallet and stumbled away from the counter, his mind whirling.

'Mary,' he gasped, reaching their table. 'Mary, we need to find Detective Bronson. Now.'

Mary looked up, alarmed by the urgency in Ted's voice. 'Ted, what's wrong? What's happened?'

'The coffee shop staff,' Ted explained hurriedly, helping Mary to her feet. 'Their badges. They all have smiley faces on them.'

Understanding dawned on Mary's face, her eyes widening with a mixture of hope and fear. Without another word, they rushed out of the coffee shop.

The journey back to Detective Bronson's temporary office in the hospital seemed to take an eternity. When they finally burst through the door, slightly out of breath, Bronson looked up from her paperwork, her eyebrows raised in surprise.

'Mr and Mrs Brown. How can I help?'

Ted, still breathless, managed to explain his discovery. As he spoke, he watched Bronson's expression change from confusion to intense focus.

'The coffee shop,' Bronson muttered, almost to herself. 'Of course. It's the perfect cover. Always busy, people coming and going at all hours...'

She turned to her partner. 'Johnson, get down to that coffee shop. I want background checks on every employee, past and present. And get me the CCTV footage from the past month.'

As Johnson hurried out, Bronson turned back to Ted and Mary. 'This could be the break we've been looking for. But it raises so many questions. Why the coffee shop? And who was the man following you? And the woman with the baby?'

Mary sank into a chair as the implications washed over her. The mundane setting of a hospital coffee shop somehow made the calculated nature of their daughter's abduction more horrifying. Someone had watched, planned, waited.

As they sat there, the room buzzing with renewed activity and purpose, Ted couldn't shake the feeling that they were on the cusp of something big. The puzzle pieces were starting to fall into place, but the picture they were forming was more complex and frightening than any of them could have imagined.

As evening settled over the hospital, Bronson's temporary office hummed with renewed purpose. Computers processed data, phones buzzed with updates, and somewhere in the building's vast network of CCTV footage, answers waited to be discovered.

In the coffee shop below, the evening shift continued their work, unaware they were now under surveillance. A barista with bright blue hair served lattes and cappuccinos, her badge gleaming under fluorescent lights.

'THE BLAME GAME'

Once filled with joyous anticipation for the twins' arrival, the Brown house now stood silent and oppressive. The air hung heavy with unspoken accusations and palpable grief.

Ted paced the living room, his eyes bloodshot from lack of sleep. Maps and timelines covered every surface, a desperate attempt to make sense of the senseless. His fingers trembled as he pinned another photo to the wall, his daughter's smiling face a stark reminder of what they'd lost.

Ted's obsessive documentation of potential leads contrasted sharply with Mary's stillness. While he pinned grainy CCTV images to walls with trembling fingers, she sat motionless in the nursery's rocking chair, time marking itself in the gentle creak of wooden runners against floor.

'Mary?' Ted's voice, hoarse from countless phone calls and pleas for information, broke the silence. 'I think I've found something.'

Mary looked up, hope and fear warring in her eyes. 'What is it?'

Ted held out a grainy security camera image, his excitement palpable. 'Look at this figure here. It could be—'

'Ted,' Mary interrupted softly, her voice cracking. 'It's just a shadow. Please... I can't take another false lead.'

The weight of her words hung between them, a chasm of shared pain and growing frustration.

'I'm trying, Mary. I'm doing everything I can to find her,' Ted's voice rose, desperation seeping through.

'And you think I'm not?' Mary shot back, suddenly on her feet. 'Every moment, every breath is for her. But chasing shadows won't bring her home!'

Their argument escalated, and years of love and trust buckled under the strain of unimaginable loss. Accusations flew, each word a dagger to already wounded hearts.

A knock at the door silenced them both. Rose and Edna entered cautiously, bearing casseroles and concerned looks.

'We thought you could use some food,' Rose offered, her eyes darting between her daughter and son-in-law.

'And maybe a breather,' Edna added, setting down her dish. 'You both look exhausted. I can take George for a while.'

'Noone will be taking George.'

'Not *take*…you know what I mean - help you, allow you to relax.'

THE GRANDMOTHERS' presence, once a source of light competition, now served as a painful reminder of the family moments their granddaughter was missing.

The silence was deafening as they sat around the dining table, the untouched food growing cold. Mary pushed her plate away, nausea rising, and went to sit on the sofa.

Mary's body was curled in on itself, arms wrapped tightly around her chest as if she were holding something fragile inside. The late afternoon sun filtered through the curtains, casting long shadows across the room. Her face, once full of warmth and laughter, now seemed hollowed out by exhaustion. Tears slipped silently down her cheeks, her voice barely a whisper.

'I can't do this, Mum,' she choked, her words trembling. 'I can't pretend everything's normal when she's out there somewhere... alone, scared. Every second feels like she's slipping further away.'

Rosie sat beside her daughter, the quiet between them heavy, almost unbearable. Her heart ached for Mary—her beautiful, broken girl. Gently, she reached out, placing a hand on Mary's knee, grounding her. She didn't rush her words; she knew Mary was delicate, teetering on the edge of breaking completely.

'I know, love. I can't imagine the pain you're feeling, but maybe... maybe you don't have to carry it alone,' Rosie's voice was soft. 'I was thinking, maybe... a support group might help. There's one in the church hall, not far. I've heard it can be a good place to share... to not feel so isolated. It might be worth trying.'

Mary shook her head, her lips pressing into a hard line, resisting. 'No, it's not for me. I don't need to sit in a room full of strangers, listening to their stories when all I want is her back.'

Rosie swallowed, her eyes filling with quiet understanding. She knew the resistance, the fear of facing this unimaginable loss. But she also knew how alone Mary had been, how she'd walled herself off, keeping the pain close as if it were her only tether to her daughter.

'It's not about them,' Rosie whispered, squeezing her hand a little tighter. 'It's about you, about finding some way to breathe again, even just for a moment. You don't have to say anything. You don't have to be ready. But... sometimes, just being with people who understand, who've felt the same kind of ache... it might not heal the wound, but it could ease it, even just a little.'

The room fell into stillness, the weight of Rosie's words sinking into the spaces between them. Mary's breath hitched, her gaze falling to the floor as a fresh wave of tears welled up.

THE CHURCH BASEMENT where the support group met was a study in faded comfort. Scuffed linoleum floors bore witness to years of shuffling feet, while mismatched chairs formed a haphazard circle under the harsh glare of fluorescent lights. The air hung heavy with the smell of lemon-scented cleaning products, a futile attempt to mask the underlying mustiness.

Mary hesitated at the doorway, gripping the worn wooden frame like a lifeline. The low murmur of voices within seemed to ebb and flow like a tide, threatening to pull her under. She closed her eyes, drawing in a shaky breath that tasted of dust and desperation.

'You can do this,' she whispered to herself, the words barely audible over the pounding of her heart.

As she stepped into the room, a dozen pairs of eyes turned towards her. Mary felt naked under their collective gaze, exposed in a way that made her want to turn and flee. But beneath the weight of their scrutiny, she saw something else – recognition. These people knew her pain and carried it within themselves like a second heartbeat.

Mary lowered herself into an empty chair. As introductions were made, she found herself studying the faces around her. A kaleidoscope of grief in various stages – raw and bleeding, scarred over, carefully hidden behind masks of forced optimism.

Mary listened to their stories as the meeting progressed – birthdays uncelebrated, milestones missed, empty beds and aching arms. Each tale was a mirror, reflecting her own pain back at her with such clarity that it stole her breath. She felt a conflicting sense of connection and isolation, grateful for their understanding yet resentful of the circumstances that brought them together.

It was Mandy, a mother whose infant son had been taken three years ago, who finally broke through Mary's carefully constructed walls. Mandy's hands, adorned with a delicate butterfly tattoo on the wrist, trembled as she spoke, her voice barely rising above a whisper.

'The guilt,' Mandy confessed, her eyes fixed on some distant point, 'it eats at you, doesn't it? Like acid, burning away at your insides until you're hollow.'

Mary felt something crack within her chest, a dam breaking. Tears spilled over, hot and relentless, carving paths down her cheeks. 'Me too. It's the guilt. I handed my baby to a stranger,' she choked out, the words tasting of bile and self-loathing. 'How could I have been so trusting? So stupid?'

Mandy reached out, grasping Mary's hand. Her grip was firm, anchoring. 'We can't live in the 'what ifs,' love. That path leads nowhere good. We have to believe they'll come home. It's the only way to keep breathing.'

As the meeting drew to a close, Mary lingered. The weight on her chest felt marginally lighter, as if sharing her burden had somehow lessened it. She wasn't alone in this nightmare – the thought was comforting and terrifying.

Outside, the world seemed too bright, too loud. Mary squinted against the setting sun's glare, her eyes sore and swollen from crying. As she walked to her car, she noticed things she'd overlooked before – a child's abandoned skipping rope on a nearby lawn, a tricycle chained to a fence, and a brightly coloured poster, advertising a music concert, fluttering in the breeze. Each sight was a reminder that life was going on all around her.

Meanwhile, across town, Ted faced a battle of his own. He stood on the porch of their home, keys in hand when a voice called out from the street.

'Mr. Brown! Mr. Brown, could I have a moment of your time?'

Ted turned to see a woman hurrying up the path, her high heels clicking against the pavement with metronomic precision. Her perfectly coiffed hair and crisp blazer marked her as out of place in their quiet, residential street.

'I'm Sarah Jameson, from the Daily Chronicle,' she said, thrusting a manicured hand towards him. Her smile was wide, predatory, her eyes gleaming with the promise of a sensational story. 'I was hoping I could ask you a few questions about your daughter's disappearance.'

'I'm sorry, but we are not making any statements,' he said, his voice rough with fatigue.

The reporter's smile didn't falter. If anything, it grew sharper. 'I understand this is a difficult time, Mr. Brown,' she said, her voice dripping with false sympathy. 'But the public has a right to know. How do you respond to rumours that you or your wife might be involved in your daughter's disappearance?'

The accusation hit Ted like a physical blow, driving the air from his lungs. The world tilted sideways for a moment, sounds becoming muffled as if he were underwater. Then, with a rush, everything snapped back into focus. Rage, hot and blinding, surged through him.

Before he could stop himself, his hands were on the reporter's shoulders, shoving her backwards. She stumbled, her heel catching in a crack in the path, sending her sprawling onto the lawn.

Horror replaced anger as Ted realised what he'd done. 'I'm sorry,' he mumbled, slumping against the porch railing. The fight drained out of him, leaving nothing but bone-deep exhaustion. 'I'm just... I'm so tired.'

The reporter scrambled to her feet, brushing grass from her skirt. For a moment, Ted thought he saw a flicker of genuine empathy in her eyes. But then her professional mask slid back into place, and she backed away, already dictating notes into her phone.

That night, the Brown house was cloaked in a suffocating silence. Mary and Ted retreated to separate rooms, the physical distance between them a pale reflection of the emotional chasm that had opened up.

In the nursery, Mary rocked back and forth in the chair that should have cradled her and her daughter. She clutched George to her chest, his soft hair damp with her tears. A broken lullaby fell from her lips, the melody distorted by sobs she could no longer contain.

Down the hall, Ted lay on his back, staring at the ceiling. The shadows cast by passing cars danced across the room, creating patterns that his exhausted mind twisted into accusing faces. Tears slid silently down his temples, soaking into the pillow beneath his head.

As the clock on the bedside table ticked, both Mary and Ted reached for their phones. They hovered over each other's contact information, fingers trembling with the desire to connect. They were so close, separated by mere walls, yet the gap between them felt insurmountable. Each was desperate to bridge the distance but unsure how to take the first step.

As dawn broke, Mary and Ted found themselves drawn to the kitchen. They moved around each other in a careful dance, brewing coffee and toasting bread in a semblance of normalcy that felt both comforting and painfully wrong.

'I went to a support group yesterday,' Mary said softly,

breaking the silence. Her voice was hoarse from crying, but there was a new strength underlying the words.

Ted looked up, a flicker of hurt crossing his face. 'I know. Your mum said that's where you were. Why didn't you ask me to come?'

Mary shrugged, her gaze fixed on the swirling patterns in her coffee. 'I didn't know how. We've been so... distant. I wasn't sure you'd want to come.'

'UNEXPECTED ALLIES'

The bell above the door of Joe's Café tinkled softly as Mary Brown stepped inside, the familiar sound a stark contrast to the unfamiliar scene that greeted her. The usually quaint and quiet establishment had transformed into a hive of activity, humming with purposeful energy.

The rich aroma of freshly brewed coffee mingled with the hearty scent of Bob the Butcher's famous beef stew, creating an oddly comforting atmosphere despite the circumstances. Mary scanned the room, taking in the faces of friends and neighbours who had come together in her family's darkest hour.

Bob stood behind a makeshift serving station, his broad shoulders hunched slightly as he ladled steaming portions of stew into bowls. His white apron was stained with splashes of broth, and his usually jovial face was set in lines of determination. A warm smile broke through his serious expression as he looked up and caught Mary's eye.

'Mary, love,' he called out, his deep voice carrying easily over the low murmur of conversation. 'Come and have a bowl. You need to keep your strength up.'

Mary made her way to him, navigating around tables cluttered with maps and laptops. The wooden floorboards creaked beneath her feet, a familiar sound that seemed amplified in her heightened state of awareness.

'Thank you, Bob,' she said softly, accepting the warm bowl. 'I don't know what we'd do without all of you.'

Bob's large hand, calloused from years of wielding butcher knives, gently patted her shoulder. 'Now, none of that,' he said gruffly, though his eyes were kind. 'we are all here for you and Ted. And we are not stopping until we bring your little girl home.'

Mary nodded, not trusting herself to speak past the lump in her throat. She turned away, cradling the bowl, and pushed the pram towards a nearby table.

From her vantage point, she could see Rick from the Antiques shop hunched over a notebook on a table. His silver hair caught the light from the overhead lamp, creating a halo effect as he leaned in, squinting through his reading glasses. The notebook was covered in a web of red lines and circles, marking areas already searched and potential leads.

Rick looked up, his keen eyes spotting Mary. He straightened, wincing slightly as he rubbed his lower back, and made his way over to her table. Up close, the lines on his face seemed deeper than Mary remembered, etched with worry and determination.

He pulled out a chair and sat down, spreading a map between them. His finger traced the marked areas as he spoke. 'Andy and Dave have been organising teams to cover the whole area. They've got the CCTV images and they're talking to everyone they can find.'

Mary leaned in, studying the map. Their town's familiar streets and landmarks, usually so comforting, now seemed alien and threatening. Each unmarked area represented a place her daughter might be, scared and alone. She swallowed hard, pushing back the fear that threatened to overwhelm her.

'Thank you, Rick,' she managed, her voice barely above a whisper. 'Your knowledge of the area has been invaluable.'

Rick nodded, a sad smile tugging at his lips. 'Been here all my life,' he said. 'Never thought I'd be using that knowledge for something like this. But we'll find her, Mary. This whole town is behind you.'

As if to emphasise his point, Andy appeared at their table, a steaming mug of tea in his hands. He set it down in front of Mary, the delicate floral scent a stark contrast to the hearty stew.

'Thought you could use this,' he said, running a hand through his messy brown hair. 'It's chamomile. Might help calm your nerves a bit.'

Mary wrapped her hands around the warm mug, grateful for its comforting heat. 'Thank you, Andy. You and Dave have been amazing.'

Andy shook his head, dismissing her thanks. 'It's the least we can do. Dave's been coordinating with the neighbouring towns, seeing if we can expand the search radius. And his sister - you remember Julie? Used to be a police dispatcher? She's been manning the hotline we set up.'

Mary nodded, remembering the friendly woman with Dave's infectious laugh. The thought of Julie's calm, capable voice fielding calls brought a small measure of comfort.

The café door opened again, bringing with it a gust of cool air and the sound of rain starting to fall outside. Ted stepped in, shaking water from his jacket. He immediately sought out Mary. The relief on his face when he spotted her was palpable.

He made his way over, stopping to accept handshakes and words of encouragement from the volunteers he passed. His hair was damp from the rain, curling slightly at the nape of his neck.

'Any news?' Mary asked, trying to keep the desperation from her voice. She knew if there had been anything significant, he would have called immediately, but she couldn't help asking.

Ted shook his head, pulling up a chair next to her. 'Nothing concrete,' he said, his voice rough with fatigue. 'But we are not giving up. The whole town is with us, Mary.'

As if to emphasise his point, a sudden burst of activity near the café's front window caught their attention. Sarah, a local IT specialist who had set up a bank of computers to monitor social media and online forums, stood up abruptly, her chair scraping loudly against the floor.

'We've got a potential sighting,' she announced, her voice cutting through the low hum of conversation. The café fell silent, all eyes turning to her. Sarah's fingers flew across her keyboard, her face illuminated by the blue glow of her screen. 'About 30 miles north. A woman matching the description was seen at a gas station.'

The room erupted into action. Rick grabbed his keys, ready to lead the way with his knowledge of the area's back roads. Andy and Dave were on their phones, coordinating with neighbouring towns to expand the search.

Mary felt her heart racing, hope and fear warring in her chest. She turned to Ted, seeing her own complex mix of emotions reflected in his eyes.

'It might be nothing,' he said softly, squeezing her hand.

'But it's something.'

They watched as a team quickly assembled. John, the local handyman, checked flash lights and radios. Milly, a nurse from the nearby clinic, packed a first aid kit. Even Mrs. Fitzgerald, well into her seventies, was there, pressing brown paper bags of sandwiches into volunteers' hands.

The air in the café was charged with a renewed sense of purpose. The smell of rain and damp earth drifted in each time the door opened. The sound of rain pattering against the windows provided a constant backdrop to the flurry of activity.

As the search team prepared to head out, Mary found herself enveloped in a warm hug. She looked up to see Lisa, her next-door neighbour, her kind face etched with concern.

'we are all praying for your little girl,' Lisa said, her voice thick with emotion. 'And we are here for you and Ted, whatever you need.'

Mary nodded, unable to speak past the lump in her throat. She watched as Lisa joined the outgoing search team, zipping up a bright yellow rain jacket.

Ted's arm slipped around her waist, and Mary leaned into him, drawing strength from his presence and the determination of the community surrounding them. She and Ted had become so distant, but she knew it was only because they were hurting so much. She needed to make an effort to get their relationship back on track...for George's sake. And her's.

As the search team filed out, the bell above the door chiming with each exit, Mary and Ted shared a look of cautious optimism. The kindness and dedication of their neighbours had become a beacon of light in their darkest hour.

The café settled into a quieter rhythm as the search team departed. Those left behind turned their attention to other tasks—manning phones, updating social media, and preparing for the next shift of volunteers.

Mary sank back into her chair, suddenly aware of how exhausted she was. The adrenaline that had been keeping her going was starting to ebb, leaving her feeling drained.

Dave approached their table, two fresh mugs of tea in his

hands. 'Thought you could use a refill,' he said, setting the steaming cups down. His face was drawn with fatigue, but his eyes were kind. 'Why don't you two try to get some rest? We've got things covered here for a while.'

Ted nodded gratefully, but Mary shook her head. 'I can't,' she said, her voice barely above a whisper. 'Not while she's out there.'

Dave's expression softened with understanding. 'I know,' he said gently. 'But you need to keep your strength up. For her.'

The door opened again, bringing with it a gust of cool, damp air. A young police officer stepped in, shaking rain from his uniform. He made his way directly to Mary and Ted, his face serious but not grim.

'Mr. and Mrs. Brown,' he said, pulling up a chair. 'I'm Officer Parker. I wanted to update you personally on the investigation.'

Mary felt Ted's hand find hers under the table, their fingers intertwining. She took a deep breath, steeling herself for whatever news the officer might bring.

Officer Parker began to speak, outlining the steps and resources allocated to the search, Mary found herself overwhelmed by a wave of gratitude. This officer, these neighbours, this entire community were all fighting for her daughter, refusing to give up hope.

As NIGHT SETTLED over the café, the rain continued its gentle percussion against the windows. Inside, the glow of computer screens and determined faces created islands of light in the growing darkness. The search continued on multiple fronts—professional and volunteer, digital and physical—each effort adding to the collective determination to bring Daisy home.

The cramped café space had become something more than a local gathering spot. It represented hope made tangible through community action, proof that in the darkest moments, light could be found in the combined efforts of ordinary people refusing to give up.

'THE TRAIL GROWS COLD'

Detective Inspector Bronson leaned closer to the monitor, her reflection ghosting across grainy CCTV footage. The images flickered in the darkened room, each frame potentially holding the key they'd been seeking.

'There,' she said, her voice carrying the quiet authority of certainty. 'Watch her movements.'

The technician leaned in closer. 'Are you certain, Detective? The image quality isn't great.'

Bronson's eyes narrowed, her gaze never leaving the screen. 'I'm sure. The build, the hair, the way she's carrying that bag all match our suspect's description.'

They watched as the woman boarded a bus, disappearing from view. Bronson's jaw tightened, her mind already racing with the implications.

'Where's that bus heading?' she asked, her voice carrying the weight of authority and urgency.

The technician's fingers flew over the keyboard. After a moment, he looked up, his expression grim. 'Millsville, it's about 120 miles away.'

Bronson inhaled sharply.

'The bus terminates in Millsville,' the technician confirmed, his fingers dancing across multiple keyboards. 'Population 12,000. Former market town, now primarily residential with surrounding woodland.'

Bronson absorbed the information with practiced efficiency. 'Alert Millsville Police. I want every CCTV feed, every potential witness statement. This woman chose that location for a reason.'

As the technician hurried to carry out her orders, Bronson turned her attention to her next task - informing the Browns.

Mary and Ted were sitting in tense silence at the Brown residence when Bronson's call came through.

Ted answered, his hand shaking slightly as he put the phone on speaker. Mary's grip on Ted's arm tightened as Bronson explained the situation.

'Millsville,' Ted repeated, his voice hoarse. 'That's... that's quite far.'

'Yes, it is,' Bronson confirmed, her tone professional but not unkind. 'we are coordinating with local law enforcement there. But I want to be clear - this lead, while promising, is not a guarantee. we are pursuing it with everything we have, but I need you both to be prepared for the possibility that it might not pan out.'

Mary nodded, even though Bronson couldn't see her. 'We understand,' she said softly. 'Thank you for keeping us informed, Detective.'

After the call ended, Mary sat quietly, and then, with a sudden burst of energy, she stood. 'We should go there,' she said, her voice filled with determination. 'To Millsville. We can help with the search.'

Ted looked up at her, concern etched on his face. 'Are you sure? It's a long trip, and Detective Bronson said they're handling it...'

SHE'S STOLEN MY BABY

'I'm sure,' Mary insisted. 'I can't just sit here waiting. I need to do something, Ted. I need to feel like we are actively looking for her.'

Ted nodded slowly, understanding dawning in his eyes. 'Okay,' he said, standing up. 'Let's go.'

They packed quickly, the act of doing anything providing a small measure of relief from the constant worry. Then they loaded George's car seat and sat their precious baby boy into it.

The journey to Millsville carved through England's changing landscape—suburban sprawl giving way to agricultural patchwork, then dense woodland embracing the approaching town. Mary watched the transformation through the passenger window, each mile marking distance from home but possibly closer to Daisy.

Millsville presented itself as almost deliberately picturesque, its High Street lined with independent shops whose hanging baskets seemed to deny the possibility of darkness.

It seemed an unlikely location for their desperate search.

They checked into a small B&B on the outskirts of town, the receptionist's curious glances making it clear that newcomers were a rarity here. In their room, Mary and Ted called Detective Bronson, who put them in touch with the local detective inspector, Clyde Harrison.

Detective Inspector Harrison embodied rural law enforcement—his weathered face and careful speech suggesting someone who knew every corner of his jurisdiction.

Mary and Ted went to meet him at the local cafe. He stood up on their arrival, his weathered face creased with sympathy. 'Mr. and Mrs. Brown,' he said, shaking their hands firmly. 'I want you to know that we are taking this very seriously. Every officer in my department has been briefed, and we are working closely with Detective Bronson's team.'

Over cups of coffee that grew cold and untouched, Harrison outlined the steps they were taking—canvassing the area around the bus station, interviewing locals, and checking security footage from local businesses. Mary and Ted listened intently.

The next few days passed in a blur of activity. Mary and Ted joined search parties, handed out flyers, and spoke to countless locals. They chased down every lead, no matter how unlikely, their desperation growing with each dead end.

On their third day in Millsville, Mary and Ted went for a walk to the local farmer's market. They were browsing pickles, chutneys and jams when Mary glimpsed her..a woman with blonde hair, similar build, even wearing clothes like those in the security footage. For a moment, time seemed to stand still.

But as the woman turned, reality came crashing back. While similar in appearance, this was clearly not their kidnapper. The woman, seeing their crestfallen expressions, offered a sympathetic smile. 'Are you alright?' she asked gently. 'You look like you've had quite a shock.'

Mary managed a weak smile in return. 'we are... we are looking for someone,' she explained, her voice barely above a whisper. 'We thought... for a moment...'

Understanding dawned in the woman's eyes. 'Oh, you poor dears,' she said softly. 'I've seen the flyers. I'm so sorry I'm not who you're looking for.'

As they trudged back to their B&B, the weight of another false lead hung heavy on their shoulders. The initial media frenzy had died down, the press pack dwindling to a single, bored-looking intern from the local paper.

'I guess the world's moving on,' Mary said quietly, her voice barely audible over the sound of their footsteps.

Ted nodded, unable to find words of comfort in the face of this stark reality. Their daughter's disappearance, once front-page news, was fading into the background, just another sad story in a world full of them.

The drive back home was subdued, the spark of hope that had fuelled their impromptu road trip now extinguished. As they pulled into their driveway, the sight of wilted flowers and outdated well-wishes on their porch served as a poignant reminder of how much time had passed.

In the living room, Mary's gaze fell on the stack of birth announcements they'd never had a chance to send out. She picked one up, her fingers tracing the embossed letters.

'We never even got to send these,' she whispered, her voice cracking. 'We were so excited to tell everyone, and now...'

The dam finally broke. Weeks of fear, hope, disappointment, and bone-deep exhaustion came pouring out in a torrent of tears. Mary collapsed into Ted's arms, her body shaking with sobs.

Ted held her close, his own tears falling silently. They stood like that for a long time, clinging to each other in their empty house, surrounded by reminders of a celebration that never came to pass.

As the sun set outside, casting long shadows across their living room, Mary and Ted remained locked in their embrace. They were back where they started, no closer to finding their daughter. But at least they were together with their son.

As Mary's sobs subsided, Ted gently cupped her face in his hands. 'Hey,' he said softly, his voice rough with emotion, 'remember what we promised each other? we are not giving up. Not ever.'

Mary nodded, drawing a shaky breath. 'You're right. We

can't.' She squared her shoulders, a flicker of her old determination returning to her eyes. 'So what's our next move?'

Ted managed a small smile. 'Well, first, I think we need to regroup. Call Detective Bronson and see if there's anything new on her end. Then we'll come up with a new plan.'

In her office, Detective Bronson studied the Millsville footage again. Something about the suspect's confidence, her careful selection of this particular destination, suggested deeper planning. This wasn't a random choice—Millsville held significance. The question was: why?

'A GLIMMER IN THE DARK'

Six months had passed. One hundred and eighty-two days of anguish, hope, and crushing disappointment. For Mary and Ted Brown, it felt like both an eternity and the blink of an eye since their daughter had been taken, leaving a gaping void in their lives that no amount of support or investigation could fill.

In the first weeks, their stories dominated headlines, and their faces constantly appeared on news broadcasts. But as days turned to weeks and weeks to months, the world moved on. Their daughter's disappearance became just another tragic story, relegated to occasional updates and human interest pieces.

This gradual slip from public consciousness was a cruel reminder of their new reality. While the world continued turning, their lives remained frozen in that terrible moment when they realised their baby was gone. Each day without her was a struggle, a battle against despair and the temptation to give up hope.

In an effort to preserve their marriage amidst this ongoing nightmare, Mary and Ted found themselves in the office of Dr

Ican, a family therapist recommended by their support group. The office was tastefully decorated in soothing tones, with comfortable seating and subtle artwork adorning the walls.

Dr Ican, a woman in her fifties with kind eyes and a calm demeanour, greeted them warmly. 'Mary, Ted, thank you for coming. I know this isn't easy, but I'm here to help you navigate this difficult time together.'

As they settled into their seats, the weight of their grief was palpable. Mary's hands trembled slightly while Ted's jaw was set in a tight line, tension evident in every line of his body.

'Now,' Dr Ican began, her voice gentle but firm, 'I'd like us to try a role reversal exercise. Mary, I want you to speak as Ted and Ted, you'll speak as Mary. The goal is to gain insight into each other's perspective.'

Mary and Ted exchanged a look, both hesitant but willing to try. Ted spoke first, his voice soft as he tried to channel Mary's thoughts. 'I'm constantly worried, every moment filled with fear for our daughter. I feel like I'm drowning in this endless search.'

Mary, speaking as Ted, responded, 'I'm trying to be strong, to keep pushing forward, but sometimes it feels hopeless. I want to protect my family, but I don't know how.'

As they continued the exercise, raw emotions bubbled to the surface. Tears flowed freely as they expressed fears and frustrations they had been holding back from each other. Dr Ican guided them gently, helping them navigate the complex landscape of their shared grief.

By the end of the session, something had shifted between them. It wasn't a magical fix but a small crack in the wall of pain that had separated them. As they left Dr Ican's office, Mary reached for Ted's hand, a gesture of connection they desperately needed.

Meanwhile, Detective Sarah Bronson was burning the midnight oil at the police station. Her desk was covered in case files, photos, and maps. Despite the case growing cold, she refused to let it slip to the back burner.

Across town, Mary sat at her computer, scrolling through old news articles about their daughter's disappearance. A ping from her email caught her attention:

'I have information about your baby. Come alone to the abandoned warehouse on Maple Street tomorrow at midnight. Tell no one, or you'll never see your child again.'

Mary called for Ted, her voice shaking. As he read the email, his face paled. 'Mary, we can't. This is a trap. We need to call Detective Bronson.'

But Mary's eyes blazed with desperate hope. 'What if it's real, Ted? What if this is our chance to find her?'

Their argument was interrupted by a call from Detective Bronson. As they relayed the contents of the email, Bronson's voice was filled with concern and determination.

'Mr. and Mrs. Brown, I understand your desire to act on this, but it's extremely dangerous. However, we can use this to our advantage. With your cooperation, we can set up a sting operation.'

The next 24 hours were a whirlwind of preparation and mounting tension. Mary was fitted with a wire, her hands shaking as the technician explained how it worked. Ted paced the room, torn between fear for his wife's safety and hope that this might lead them to their daughter.

As midnight approached, Mary found herself standing before the looming warehouse. Her heart raced, each beat seeming to echo in the quiet night. Behind her, hidden in vans and surrounding buildings, were Ted, Detective Bronson, and a team of officers, all poised to act at a moment's notice.

Taking a deep breath, Mary reached for the door handle. 'Please,' she whispered, a prayer to anyone listening, 'let this be the break we've been waiting for.'

With one last glance back at where she knew Ted was watching, Mary stepped into the darkness of the warehouse. The door creaked shut behind her, sealing her into whatever fate awaited inside.

As Mary disappeared from view, Ted felt his heart constrict with fear and hope. Detective Bronson placed a reassuring hand on his shoulder, her voice low and determined. 'We've got eyes and ears on her, Mr. Brown. Your wife is incredibly brave, and we are going to do everything in our power to keep her safe and hopefully, bring your daughter home.'

The warehouse door's creak carried clearly through Mary's wire, its sound marking transition from known to unknown. As darkness swallowed her form, Bronson's team tensed like coiled springs, ready for whatever might emerge from this midnight gambit.

In the van, Ted pressed his hand against the monitor showing Mary's last visible position, his wedding ring catching light from the screens. Behind him, Bronson spoke quietly into her radio, confirming positions, maintaining control of an operation balanced on knife's edge.

THE TWIST

The warehouse air hung thick with decades of abandonment, its musty perfume mingling with traces of rust and decay. Mary's footsteps echoed against concrete, each sound amplified by the cavernous space. Moonlight filtered through broken windows, creating silver pathways through darkness.

'Hello?' she called out, her voice echoing in the cavernous space. 'Is anyone there?'

A figure emerged from the shadows, moving slowly and deliberately. 'Mary,' a voice said, 'I'm so glad you came.'

Mary squinted, trying to make out the person's features. There was something about that voice, something that tugged at her memory. 'Step into the light,' Mary said, her voice steady despite her racing heart.

The figure obliged, stepping forward into a shaft of moonlight streaming through a broken window. Mary gasped, her eyes widening in recognition. 'Nurse Joy?' she exclaimed, her voice a mixture of surprise and confusion. 'Where's my baby? Why did you take her? What's going on? Are you even a nurse at all?'

'No. I'm a sister.'

'A ward sister?'

'No, I'm Richard's sister.'

'Who's Richard?'

'Oh, come on now. You know very well who Richard is.'

'I don't. I don't know what you're talking about. Where is my baby girl?'

'The way you treated my brother was appalling.'

'I don't know your brother. None of this makes any sense at all.'

'Yes, you do.'

'This is insane. Just tell me where my daughter is.'

Mary took a cautious step forward, acutely aware of the wire hidden beneath her clothing. 'Joy, what did you do? Where is my daughter?'

'It was revenge for the way you treated him. That's all. It just went a bit far.'

'A bit far?'

'It was just supposed to scare you. We were going to give her back but the police were there and journalists were there. How could we give the baby back when five minutes after we took her the place was surrounded?'

'What? So you kept her for six months? You've put me through six months of hell. WHERE IS SHE?'

'Well, I. You. I mean...'

As Joy's words devolved into incoherent mumbling, Mary became aware of movement behind her. Detective Bronson and a team of officers had entered silently, their weapons drawn but lowered.

Joy's head snapped up at the interruption, her eyes widening in panic. 'You brought the police? You promised to come alone!'

Detective Bronson stepped forward, her voice calm but

authoritative. 'Joy, we need you to tell us where the baby is. If you cooperate, this can end peacefully.'

For a moment, it seemed like Joy might try to run. But then her shoulders sagged in defeat. 'She's in a cabin in the woods,' Joy said, her voice barely above a whisper. 'My sister is caring for her.'

The next few minutes passed in a blur of activity. Mary stood rooted to the spot. Her daughter was alive. She was going to get her back.

Joy was led away in handcuffs, alternating between sobbing apologies and muttering about cosmic justice.

'Come on, let's go,' said Bronson, leaving Joy to her team of officers.

As the unmarked police car wound through dark forest roads, Mary reached out and grasped Ted's hand. They were close. So close to their daughter.

The car came to a stop in front of a rustic cabin. As Mary and Ted approached the front door, hearts pounding, they were acutely aware of the magnitude of this moment. Beyond this door could be their baby and the end of their nightmare.

They stood back while a Firearms Command team prepared to enter.

Taking a deep breath, an officer raised his fist and knocked. The sound echoed through the night, seeming to hang in the air like a question mark.

For a moment, there was silence. Then, from inside, came a sound that made Mary's heart stop and restart with the force of a jackhammer.

A baby's cry.

Their daughter's cry?

Police officers spread around the cabin, and Mary and Ted stood frozen, overwhelmed by emotions. The night air was thick with tension and the promise of a long-awaited resolution.

Seconds later, the police charged in, their weapons drawn and voices raised in a cacophony of shouted commands.

'Police! Don't move!'

'Hands where we can see them!'

'Get down on the ground, now!'

The chaos was immediate and overwhelming. Mary moved forward but felt a strong hand grasp her arm, yanking her backwards. She stumbled, her eyes still locked on the cot in the middle of the room, as an officer pulled her to safety. Ted was at her side instantly, his arm wrapping protectively around her shoulders as they were ushered away from the scene.

'OK,' shouted one of the officers. 'Mary and Ted - you can come in now.'

The officer's invitation to enter carried the weight of months of separation. Mary and Ted stood at the threshold of either reunion or renewed heartbreak, the moment balanced on a knife's edge of possibility.

Beyond the door, a child's cry continued—familiar yet changed by time and circumstance. Mary's hand found Ted's again as they prepared to step forward into whatever reality awaited them.

REUNITED

The door of the cabin opened with a creak that seemed to echo the tension of the moment. Mary and Ted entered cautiously, their hearts pounding in unison. The interior was a stark contrast to the rustic exterior, filled with an abundance of baby paraphernalia that spoke of careful, if misguided, preparation.

In the centre of the room stood a woman who could only be Nurse Joy's sister. Her eyes widened with panic as she saw Mary and Ted, instinctively tightening her hold on the baby in her arms.

'Please,' Mary said, her voice trembling with emotion, 'that's my baby.'

The woman's face crumpled, a mix of fear and resignation washing over her features. 'I... I can explain. I was just trying to help my brother. I didn't know this was going to happen.'

An officer moved slowly, deliberately placing himself between the woman and the door. 'It's over now. Hand back the baby.'

For a moment, it seemed as if the woman might try to

run. But then her shoulders sagged, the fight leaving her. Gently, she placed the baby in the officers arms.

Mary rushed forward, her eyes never leaving the tiny face she'd been longing to see for six agonising months. With trembling hands, she lifted her daughter, cradling her close. Ted was right behind her.

'Oh, my darling,' Mary whispered, tears streaming down her face. 'My beautiful, perfect baby.'

Ted's arms encircled them both, his own tears falling freely. 'We found you,' he murmured, his voice thick with emotion. 'We found you.'

The baby, as if sensing the monumental nature of the moment, began to coo and reach out with tiny hands.

The tender moment was interrupted by the police and paramedics. The small cabin quickly filled with activity as officers secured the scene and medical professionals moved in to check on the baby.

'Mr. and Mrs. Brown,' a paramedic said gently, 'we need to examine the baby. It's standard procedure.'

Mary nodded, reluctantly allowing the paramedic to take her daughter. Ted followed him, refusing to let his daughter out of sight. The examination was thorough but quick, both parents hovering anxiously nearby.

'She appears to be in excellent health,' the paramedic announced, much to Mary and Ted's relief. 'But we'll do a more comprehensive check at the hospital.'

As they prepared to leave, Detective Bronson approached them. 'I wanted to let you know that we are still searching for the nurse's brother, who is also involved in this. He seems to have vanished, but we won't rest until we've found him.'

Ted pulled Mary closer. 'Thank you, Detective. Please, keep us informed.'

'Do you know why they took her?' asked Mary.

Bronson shook her head.

The journey to the hospital was surreal. Mary and Ted sat in the back of an ambulance, each holding a baby, unwilling to let go even for a moment. They alternated between staring in wonder at their children and exchanging glances of disbelief and joy.

At the hospital, they were met with a flurry of activity. Doctors and nurses swarmed around them, conducting tests and asking questions.

When the doctor finally emerged with the DNA test results, his smile was reassuring: 'Congratulations, Mr. and Mrs. Brown. This is indeed your baby daughter.'

The wave of relief that washed over them was almost physical in its intensity. Mary sagged against Ted, who wrapped an arm around her shoulders, steadying them both.

As they prepared to take their baby home, they were met with a media frenzy outside the hospital. Reporters clamoured for statements; cameras flashed incessantly.

Ted, usually quick with a joke, addressed the crowd with uncharacteristic gravity. 'We are overjoyed to have our child back. We ask for privacy as we reconnect as a family. Thank you for your support during this difficult time.'

The drive home was quiet, filled with exhaustion and elation. As they pulled into their driveway, they were greeted by a sight that brought fresh tears to their eyes. Their front yard had been transformed into a welcome home celebration, with banners, balloons, and their families waiting for them.

Rose and Edna, the grandmothers, stood side by side, united in their joy. As Mary and Ted approached with the baby, the women's delighted squeals were slightly less restrained than their tearful embraces.

'Oh, look at them together,' Rose cooed, gently stroking a tiny cheek. 'They're perfect.'

Edna nodded in agreement, her eyes never leaving the babies. 'They've got Mary's nose, thank goodness.'

Ted raised an eyebrow at that, but his smile never faltered. The playful jabs were a welcome return to normalcy after months of stress and fear.

Making their way through the impromptu celebration, Mary and Ted finally reached the nursery. The room felt like a time capsule of hope and heartbreak. Gently, they placed the babies in their cots.

For a long moment, they stood there, watching their children sleep and marvelling at the miracle of their return. Ted wrapped an arm around Mary's waist, pulling her close.

'We did it,' he whispered, his voice thick with emotion. 'We did it.'

Mary nodded, leaning into him. 'I can't believe they're here. After all this time...'

As they stood there, basking in the peaceful sound of their babies' breathing, the chaos of the past six months seemed to melt away. The fear, the heartbreak, the twists and turns of their search—all of it faded into the background, leaving only this moment—this perfect, beautiful moment of family reunited.

The sounds of their family and friends came from downstairs, celebrating and preparing for the Browns' first night back as a complete family. But in this quiet nursery, Mary and Ted were content to simply watch their babies sleep, grateful beyond words for their safe return.

Questions remained—the brother's whereabouts, the full scope of motivation—but for now, watching their twins sleep side by side, Mary and Ted allowed themselves to simply exist in the perfection of reunion.

Outside their window, Detective Bronson's team maintained discreet surveillance, knowing the brother's disappearance required continued vigilance. But inside the nursery, peace reigned as a family found its way home.

MY BABY

Sleep proved elusive that first night of reunion, Mary's every nerve alive to her daughter's presence. Each breath, each tiny movement registered with crystalline clarity, as if her maternal instincts were compensating for months of enforced silence.

The weight of two babies in her arms sent a shock through her system as if her body was suddenly remembering a crucial part of itself that had been missing. She pulled her child close, inhaling deeply, drinking in the sweet, familiar scent she'd been longing for these past six agonising months.

A sob escaped her throat, and suddenly Mary found herself crying uncontrollably, her tears falling onto her daughter's soft wisps of hair. She cradled the baby's head, her fingers gently tracing the delicate curve of her cheek, the tiny button nose, the perfect bow of her lips. Each feature was a miracle, a treasure she'd feared she'd never see again.

Mary's chest heaved with each breath, her heart pounding so hard she was sure it would burst from the sheer force of her emotions. Joy, relief, disbelief - they all swirled together in a dizzying whirlwind. She pressed her lips to her daughter's forehead, the contact sending another wave of tears cascading down her cheeks.

'My baby,' she whispered, her voice hoarse and barely audible. 'My beautiful, perfect baby. You're here. You're really here.'

The baby stirred in her arms, tiny fingers curling around Mary's thumb. The simple gesture nearly brought Mary to her knees. She swayed gently, instinctively rocking her child, a motion she'd dreamed of for so long.

Time seemed to stand still as Mary drank in every detail of her daughter. The rise and fall of her chest, the flutter of her eyelashes, the soft coos that escaped her lips - each moment was precious, a gift Mary had feared was lost forever.

As the reality of the reunion settled in, Mary felt a lightness she hadn't experienced in months. The heavy cloud of grief and fear that had shadowed her every waking moment began to lift, replaced by a fierce, all-encompassing love.

Beyond their windows, London continued its nocturnal rhythms. Somewhere, Detective Bronson's team pursued their remaining questions, but here in this sanctuary of moonlight and renewed connection, Mary allowed herself to simply exist in the miracle of reunion.

Her daughter's weight in her arms anchored her to this moment, while promise of tomorrow beckoned with gentle persistence. They had time now—time to heal, time to bond, time to rebuild what had been so cruelly interrupted.

IT'S RICHARD

Detective Bronson entered the room, her face a mask of professional calm that did little to hide the tension in her shoulders. She sat across from Mary and Ted, her hands clasped tightly on the table.

'Mr. and Mrs. Brown,' she began, her voice gentle but firm, 'we've apprehended the man who was working with Joy. His name is Richard Hartley.'

Mary frowned, the name tickling at the edges of her memory. 'Richard Hartley? I don't think I know...'

'Mrs. Brown,' Bronson continued, 'Mr. Hartley claims to know you. He says you went on a date several years ago, set up by your friends Charlie and Juan through an internet dating site.'

And suddenly, like a key turning in a lock, the memories came flooding back. Mary gasped, her hand flying to her mouth.

'Oh my god. Richard. The poet. I... I'd completely forgotten.'

Ted leaned forward, his face a storm of confusion and anger. 'What? Mary, who is this guy?'

Mary's voice shook as she explained. 'It was one date, years ago, when we were having a break, and you went out with Dawn. Do you remember - I told you. Juan and Charlie set me up on all these internet dates that were completely terrible in every way. Richard was so pretentious, going on and on about obscure poets and the meaning of flowers. I never called him back.'

Bronson nodded grimly. 'Mr. Hartley has confessed to being involved in the kidnapping. He overheard you talking about your pregnancy at the restaurant. He mentioned it to his sister, Joy, who works in the hospital coffee shop. That's how they were able to gain access and... take your daughter.'

'I don't understand how someone who works in the bloody coffee shop manages to wield so much power.'

'The hospital's security infrastructure is a web of controlled access and monitored movement. Joy's position in the café had allowed her to observe the rhythms of staff changes, the precise timing of ward rotations, and the subtle patterns that governed hospital life. Over months, she had noted which doors required key card access, which corridors saw heaviest traffic, and—most crucially—which areas suffered from surveillance blind spots.'

'And she managed to pass all that information to her sister?'

'Yes. The abduction took place in a shift change—that critical period when tired staff transferred responsibilities to fresh arrivals, when usual vigilance wavered under administrative demands. She understood that temporary confusion created opportunity, that handover protocols sometimes faltered under routine's weight.'

'That's just ridiculous.'

'The hospital will write to you. They are changing and updating all security systems.'

'Good.'

'I still can't get over Richard, though. He loses his mind over one bad date?'

'According to Richard,' Bronson said softly, 'seeing Mrs Brown happy and expecting a baby brought back feelings of rejection and bitterness. He told his sister and a plan was hatched.

'He claims they wanted to scare you, but things... escalated. His other sister got involved - the lady who took the baby from you and was in the restaurant with him that night. He said he never meant that to happen. They just wanted to scare you.'

Mary shook her head, tears streaming down her face. 'I can't believe this. One date. One stupid date, and it led to all of this?'

'How does someone working in the coffee shop get to wander into a room and do a sonogram. It's insane.'

'It is,' agreed Bronson.

As Bronson continued to explain the details of Richard and Joy's confession, Mary's mind reeled. All those months of fear and heartache, the sleepless nights and desperate searches, all stemming from a single evening years ago that she'd all but forgotten. The realisation was almost too much to bear.

Outside Bronson's office, London continued its afternoon bustle, oblivious to these revelations. Yet within this space, three lives forever altered by one forgotten evening tried to reconcile past and present, action and consequence, nightmare and awakening.

THE LETTER

⁂

*D*etective Inspector Bronson's presentation of the envelope carried deliberate neutrality. Her careful handling of the missive suggested its contents might prove as volatile as any evidence she'd previously managed.

'This was given to us by Richard Hartley,' she said, her tone carefully neutral. 'He asked that we pass it on to you, Mrs. Brown. You're under no obligation to read it, of course.'

Mary stared at the envelope, her emotions warring across her face. Anger, curiosity, and fear battled for dominance. With trembling hands, she reached out and took the letter.

'You don't have to read it now,' Ted said softly, his hand on her shoulder. 'Or ever, if you don't want to.'

Mary shook her head. 'No, I... I need to know.' She took a deep breath and tore open the envelope, unfolding the pages within.

As she read, her expression shifted from anger to disbelief, then to a complex mix of emotions too tangled to name.

DEAR MARY,

My hands tremble as I write this, knowing no words can undo the pain I've caused. The weight of my actions sits heavy on my soul, a burden I'll carry for the rest of my days.

I remember our date as if it were yesterday. Your laughter, your passion for literature, the way your eyes lit up when you spoke of your dreams. For me, it wasn't just a date. It was the beginning of everything. But for you, it was nothing more than a forgettable evening.

In the years that followed, I watched from afar as you built your life. Each milestone you achieved was a dagger to my heart, a reminder of what I could never have. When I saw you at the restaurant that day, radiant with the joy of impending motherhood, something inside me shattered.

I told my sisters to make life difficult for you. A childish, spiteful request born from years of pent-up resentment and unrequited feelings. Never, in my darkest moments, did I imagine one of them would take your child. When she showed up with your baby, I was horrified. But by then, it was too late. We were in too deep.

The months that followed were a living hell. Every day, I saw the pain I'd caused reflected in your daughter's eyes. I wanted to return her, to end this madness, but fear and my sister's determination held me back.

I know these words mean little in the face of what you've endured. I don't seek forgiveness – I don't deserve it. I only hope that knowing the truth might offer you some peace.

Your daughter is beautiful, Mary. She has your spirit, your resilience. Take solace in knowing that, despite everything, she was loved and cared for.

I'm so sorry. For everything.

Richard

Mary absorbed the letter's contents in complete stillness, each word landing with physical force. The revelation of years-long observation added fresh dimension to their ordeal.

Mary's gaze was distant. The room was silent, waiting for her reaction.

'He...' she began, her voice barely above a whisper. 'He's been watching me all this time. All these years...' She trailed off, shaking her head in disbelief.

Richard's words, meant as explanation, had instead illuminated darker truth—the capacity of wounded ego to spawn devastating consequence.

'Well, now he's going to pay for it,' said Detective Bronson.

In her office, Bronson added the letter to evidence, its pages joining comprehensive documentation of obsession's evolution into action. Outside, London's autumn light cast long shadows, while inside, Mary and Ted absorbed fresh understanding of their ordeal's genesis.

THE AFTERMATH

As they stood in the nursery, watching their twins sleep peacefully in their cribs, the weight of the day's revelations hung heavy in the air. Mary's fingertips traced her daughter's features with butterfly gentleness, each touch both confirmation and celebration. Daisy's skin held that peculiar softness unique to infants, a texture that spoke directly to maternal instinct. Next, she did the same to George. They were such beautiful babies.

'I still can't believe it,' she whispered, her voice thick with emotion. 'All of this because of Richard. A man I barely knew, who I'd completely forgotten about.'

Ted moved behind her, wrapping his arms around her waist and resting his chin on her shoulder. 'Some people can't let go of the past,' he murmured. 'But we can't let what he did overshadow this moment. we are together. we are safe. That's all that matters now.'

Mary leaned back into his embrace, drawing strength from his steady presence. 'I know. It's just... when I think of how close we came to losing her, to losing everything...'

Her voice broke, and Ted tightened his hold. 'But we

didn't,' he said firmly. 'We fought, we never gave up, and now our family is whole again.'

They stood there in silence for a long moment, the only sound the soft breathing of their sleeping children. Finally, Mary turned in Ted's arms, meeting his gaze.

'You're right,' she said, a small smile tugging at her lips. 'What Richard and Joy did was unforgivable, but we can't let it define us. We have our whole lives ahead of us, as a family.'

One of the twins stirred as if on cue, letting out a tiny whimper. Mary and Ted moved as one, ready to attend to their child's needs. In that moment, surrounded by the love of her family, Mary felt the last of her fears begin to fade.

SLEEPLESS FOR NEW REASONS

Night wrapped around the Brown house like protective embrace, while inside, new patterns of parenthood played out in hushed movements. Mary and Ted's footsteps traced careful paths between nursery and bedroom, each check on their twins carrying lingering traces of recent anxiety.

Mary tiptoed into the nursery, her heart racing with each step. The soft glow of the nightlight cast gentle shadows across the room as she approached the cribs. She peered in, her eyes drinking in the sight of her sleeping children. Her breath caught in her throat as she watched the rise and fall of their tiny chests, a simple act that filled her with overwhelming relief and gratitude.

'Still here,' she whispered, her voice barely audible. 'Still safe.'

As she turned to leave, her foot caught on the edge of the plush rug. She stumbled, catching herself on the edge of the crib. The small sound was enough to bring Ted rushing to the doorway, his eyes wide with concern.

'Everything okay?' he asked softly, his voice tight with barely contained worry.

Mary nodded, offering a tired smile. 'Just me being clumsy. They're fine, still sleeping. I manage to bash my chest, though, and now my nipple's leaking.'

'Oh, Christ. That's not ideal, is it? Do you need me to help in any way? Massage it or something.'

'I don't think that would be wise. That would make it worse.'

'I might just tell you an interesting fact instead, then. Did you know that the German word for nipple is breast wart?'

'Thanks for that, Ted.'

'Do you fancy a muffin?'

'A muffin? What - now?'

'Yes. I got some that were left at work after the meeting and brought them back.'

'Well, if I'm good for anything, it's hoovering up surplus muffins. Bring 'em on.'

They sat on the sofa with a large bag of muffins between them.

'There are eight, I think,' said Ted. 'That should keep us going til morning.'

'This is all pretty wonderful, isn't it?' said Mary. 'I know we are lunatics to be up at ungodly hours eating stale muffins, but it's all good fun.'

'They're not stale; what are you talking about?' said Ted.

'They're definitely on the turn, Ted. I'm not planning to refuse to eat them, but they're far from fresh.

'And all I'm saying is - we must appreciate every minute with the twins more because of what happened, don't you think? I don't care about being woken up through the night or coping with all the mess after what happened. Whatever the future brings, if the four of us are safe, everything will be OK.'

'You're right,' said Ted, spraying muffin crumbs everywhere.

'I keep expecting to wake up and find this was all a dream,' Mary confessed, leaning into Ted's embrace. 'That she'll be gone again.'

Ted tightened his hold, pressing a kiss to her temple. 'I know. Me too. But she's here, Mary. They both are. we are all together.'

As if on cue, the baby monitor gave a soft whimper, quickly followed by a full-throated cry. Mary and Ted moved in unison, each reaching for a baby with practised ease.

THE NEXT MORNING, the doorbell rang too early for comfort.

'The police?' said Mary.

'I don't know. You stay here with the twins and I'll go and answer it,' said Ted.

He opened the door narrowly to see his mum and Rosie on the doorstep, smiling with their arms laden with food.

The grandmothers swept in, their excitement palpable.

'I have enough baked goods to feed a small army,' said Edna. 'Now, how's it all going? Are they sleeping through the night?'

'Not really. We sleep with them most nights.'

'Babies need routine,' Rose announced, already rolling up her sleeves. 'When Mary was little—'

'Actually,' Edna interrupted, unpacking her offerings, 'the latest research suggests baby-led scheduling. I was reading just yesterday that we need to be careful about imposing adult structure on babies.'

'Research!' Rose's eyebrows achieved impressive height. 'There's no substitute for experience. Now, about their sleeping arrangements—'

Mary watched this familiar dance with mixed affection

and exhaustion. 'Mum, Edna... we appreciate everything. More than you know. But right now...'

'We've been through a lot and we are still finding our feet,' Ted finished, his hand finding Mary's shoulder.

Rose paused in her grand reorganisation of their kitchen cupboards. 'Oh, darling. Of course.' Her voice softened. 'We just want to help.'

'I remember those early days,' Edna added, sinking into an armchair. 'The uncertainty. The constant worry.'

'The fear of doing everything wrong,' Rose agreed, sharing a rare moment of harmony with her co-grandmother.

'You're not doing anything wrong,' they said in unison, then shared surprised looks at their synchronicity.

CHARLIE ARRIVED LATER, bearing proper coffee and understanding. She settled into their battered sofa, watching Mary's protective hovering with quiet insight.

'Remember when we thought hangovers were life's greatest challenge?' she mused, making Mary snort into her coffee.

'Simpler times,' Mary agreed. 'Though I don't recall you being much help then either.'

'Excuse me? Who held your hair back after the infamous tequila incident of 2018?'

'The same person who suggested tequila was an appropriate Thursday night choice?'

Their shared laughter felt like old times, until Daisy stirred and Mary's attention snapped back instantly.

'Hey,' Charlie said gently, noting her friend's tension. 'They're safe, Mary. You're allowed to relax. To laugh. To be you again.'

'I know,' Mary whispered, adjusting Daisy's blanket for

the thousandth time. 'Logically, I know. But every time I close my eyes...'

'Then we'll keep them open together,' Charlie promised. 'For as long as you need.'

As the day wound down, Mary sat quietly, looking at her husband.

'we are doing okay, right?' Mary whispered, her eyes never leaving her daughter's peaceful face.

Ted nodded, stifling a yawn. 'we are doing great. Our kids are home, they're safe, and they're loved. That's what matters.'

Mary smiled. 'You're right. we are together, and that's the most important thing.'

As they sat there, gently rocking their sleeping children, Mary and Ted felt the pull of exhaustion tugging at their eyelids. They knew they should put the babies down, try to get some sleep themselves. But neither could bring themselves to let go, not yet.

And so, as the first light of dawn began to peek through the nursery curtains, Mary and Ted drifted off to sleep in their chairs, each holding a baby close. It wasn't the most comfortable sleeping arrangement, but for now, in this quiet, peaceful moment, everything was perfect.

HEALING TOGETHER

*D*r Ican's consulting room offered calculated serenity—walls in muted sage, artwork selected for its calming properties, furniture arranged to encourage openness while preserving dignity. Mary and Ted sat with practised care, each cradling a twin, their postures suggesting lingering vigilance despite professional surroundings.

Ted's eyes darted around the room, taking in the elegant decor. 'Are we admitting defeat?' His whispered question carried layers of uncertainty.

'Mary sighed, gently bouncing the fussy baby on her knee. 'I think it's admitting we need help,' she replied softly. 'And after everything we've been through, isn't that okay?'

Before Ted could respond, the office door opened, and Dr Ican stepped out. Her warm smile and gentle demeanour immediately put them at ease. 'Mr. and Mrs. Brown? Please, come in.'

As they settled into the cosy office, Dr Ican addressed their obvious tension. 'I know this isn't easy,' she said, her voice kind but firm. 'But you've taken an important step in coming here. Let's start by talking about your hopes and fears for your family.'

Ted's hand found Mary's, squeezing gently. 'I guess our biggest fear is... everything,' he admitted, his voice cracking slightly. 'We got our babies back, which is incredible. But now we are terrified of losing them again.'

Mary nodded, tears welling in her eyes. 'I see danger everywhere now. Yesterday, I nearly had a panic attack at a birthday party because a balloon popped. I'm exhausted from constantly being on alert.'

Dr Ican listened attentively, her expression compassionate. 'What you're experiencing is a normal response to trauma,' she assured them. 'Let's work on coping strategies to help you feel more secure.'

As the session progressed, Mary and Ted opened up about the fears, hopes, and challenges in their daily lives. Sensing the emotional atmosphere, the babies remained unusually calm, occasionally making soft noises that brought small smiles to their parents' faces.

Armed with Dr Ican's suggestions and a renewed sense of purpose, Mary and Ted decided to take their first 'normal' family outing to the park. The sunny day belied the storm of emotions brewing within them as they approached the playground.

Mary's eyes scanned the area, her grip on the pram tightening with each step. 'Ted,' she whispered, her voice strained, 'are you sure this is safe? There are so many people here.'

Ted, in the midst of applying sunscreen to the babies with meticulous care, paused to meet her gaze. 'We can't keep them in a bubble forever. Remember what the doctor said - we must start trusting the world again.'

Taking a deep breath, Mary nodded. 'You're right. This is supposed to be fun.'

As they settled the twins into the baby swings, their

giggles of delight seemed to cut through the anxiety. For a moment, everything was perfect. They were just a normal family enjoying a beautiful day at the park.

Then, a well-meaning stranger approached, cooing over the babies. 'Oh, what adorable twins! How old are they?'

Mary froze, her breath catching in her throat. In an instant, she was back in that hospital room, watching helplessly as a stranger walked away with her baby. The world tilted sideways, sounds becoming muffled and distorted.

Ted, recognising the signs of Mary's panic, quickly stepped in. He gently guided the stranger away with a polite excuse, then turned his attention to his wife. Taking her trembling hands in his, he spoke in a low, soothing voice.

'Mary, honey. You're safe. The babies are safe. we are in the park, remember? No one's going to take them. I've got you. Just breathe with me, okay?'

Slowly, Mary came back to herself. The park swam into focus, the sounds of children playing gradually replacing the roaring in her ears. She looked at Ted, tears streaming down her face.

'I'm sorry,' she whispered. 'I thought... I thought she was going to...'

Ted pulled her into a gentle embrace, mindful of the babies who were still happily swinging. 'Shh, it's okay. You have nothing to be sorry for. we are all still healing. It's going to take time.'

In the weeks that followed, Mary and Ted worked hard to rebuild their trust in the world and in others. They started small, allowing the grandmothers to babysit for short periods while they went for walks or had quick coffee dates.

Their first proper date night was an exercise in careful planning and barely contained anxiety. As they prepared to leave, Mary ran through a checklist for what felt like the hundredth time.

'We've got the emergency contact list, the backup list, the security system instructions...' her voice trailed off as she saw the knowing looks exchanged between Rose and Edna.

Rose stepped forward, her voice gentle but firm. 'We raised you two, remember? We can handle a few hours with our grandchildren.'

Ted, who had been doing deep breathing exercises to calm his nerves, managed a weak smile. 'You're right. we are being silly. It's just... it's our first time leaving them since...'

Edna squeezed his arm reassuringly. 'We know, sweetheart. And we understand. But you two need this. Go, enjoy your dinner. We've got everything under control here.'

Mary sat across from Ted in a quaint Italian restaurant, the kind of place they used to frequent before their world had been turned upside down. The familiar scents of garlic, basil, and freshly baked bread wafted through the air, a sensory reminder of simpler times.

Mary's fingers toyed nervously with the stem of her wine glass, her eyes darting to her phone for what felt like the hundredth time that evening. The screen remained stubbornly dark. She wasn't sure if the lack of news was reassuring or anxiety-inducing.

'They're fine, love,' Ted said softly, reaching across the table to gently squeeze her hand. His touch was warm, grounding, and Mary felt some of the tension ease from her shoulders. 'The mums have it under control.'

Mary managed a small smile, the first genuine one of the evening. 'I know. It's just...'

'I know,' Ted nodded, understanding shining in his eyes. 'But we need this. We deserve this.'

As if on cue, the waiter appeared with their starters. The sight of the beautifully presented bruschetta momentarily distracted Mary from her worries. She took a bite, closing her eyes as the flavours burst across her tongue - the sweetness of ripe tomatoes, the pungency of garlic, the freshness of basil. It was a simple pleasure, but one that seemed magnified after months of stress.

As they ate, Mary found herself studying Ted's face in the soft light. The lines of worry that had become a permanent fixture in recent months seemed less pronounced tonight. His eyes, when they met hers, held a warmth that made her breath catch. She was suddenly, acutely aware of how long it had been since they'd simply looked at each other without the weight of fear and exhaustion clouding their vision.

'Do you remember our first date after we met at Fat Club?' Ted asked, a hint of mischief in his voice. 'That awful Chinese place?'

Mary laughed, the sound surprising her with its genuineness. 'God, yes. I thought I was going to die of food poisoning. But you were so sweet, trying to make it up to me.'

'I was terrified you'd never want to see me again,' Ted admitted, his eyes crinkling at the corners as he smiled. 'I even practised my apology speech in the mirror.'

Something shifted within her as they reminisced, sharing stories and laughing over shared memories. She leaned in closer to Ted, drawn to the familiar sound of his voice, the way his hands moved animatedly as he spoke, the laughter that came so readily.

Their main courses arrived—a fragrant risotto for Mary and osso buco for Ted. As they savoured the rich, comforting flavours, their conversation flowed. They talked about their hopes for the twins' future, their dreams that had been put on hold but not forgotten. For the first time in months, they allowed themselves to look forward beyond the all-consuming present.

Halfway through the meal, Mary's phone buzzed. Her

hand darted out, her heart leaping into her throat. But it was just a photo from her mother—the twins, peacefully asleep in their cribs. Their little faces were relaxed in slumber.

'See? They're perfect,' Ted said, his voice thick with emotion as he looked at the photo. 'And they'll still be perfect when we get home. But right now, this is our time.'

Mary nodded, putting the phone away with only a slight hesitation. She took a deep breath, consciously choosing to be present in this moment with the man she loved.

As the evening progressed, Mary found herself rediscovering Ted. The gentle strength in his hands as he gestured, the slight dimple in his left cheek that only appeared with his widest smiles. It was like seeing him anew, appreciating details she had once known by heart but had somehow lost sight of in the chaos of recent months.

They lingered over dessert - a rich tiramisu that they shared, forks playfully duelling for the last bite. The coffee was strong and aromatic, its bitterness a pleasant counterpoint to the sweetness of the dessert.

As they left the restaurant, Ted took Mary's hand, interlacing their fingers. The night air was cool and crisp, carrying the scent of blooming jasmine from a nearby garden. They walked slowly, in no hurry to end the evening, their steps falling into a synchronised rhythm.

'Thank you,' Mary said softly, looking up at Ted. 'For tonight. For everything.'

Ted stopped, turning to face her. 'I love you more every day, Mary. Just when I think I couldn't love you any more, a little pop of extra love arrives.'

Mary stood on her tiptoes, kissing Ted's lips softly. The kiss spoke of renewed connection, of a love tested by fire but emerging stronger.

As they made their way home, Mary felt lighter than she had in months. The worry wasn't gone—she doubted it ever would be completely gone —but it no longer seemed all-consuming. Tonight reminded her of who they were as a couple and the strength they found in each other.

Approaching their front door, Mary paused, taking a moment to savour the anticipation of seeing their children.

'Ready?' Ted asked, his hand on the doorknob.

Mary nodded, squeezing his other hand. 'Ready.'

LEGAL BATTLES AND LULLABIES

*L*ondon sweltered under unseasonable heat as Mary stood before her bedroom mirror, fingers trembling over shirt buttons. The morning light seemed harsh and unforgiving, highlighting shadows of sleepless nights beneath her eyes.

'I don't know if I can do this, Ted,' she whispered, her voice cracking. The thought of seeing Richard and his two vile sisters again made her stomach churn, a cold sweat breaking out on her forehead.

She knew so much about what they had done now - Joy, the woman who worked in the coffee shop, used her pass to enter the building for her sister Sian. According to everything the police had told her, Richard didn't know how far the two of them would go in avenging the pain that Mary had allegedly caused him.

But, surely, he must have had an idea. And even if he didn't, why not call the police as soon as they emerged with her baby? What the hell was wrong with them all?

'What if... what if I fall apart in there?' she asked Ted.

Ted appeared behind her, his own face etched with worry.

He placed his hands on her shoulders, their eyes meeting in the mirror. 'Then we'll leave. There's no pressure.'

Outside, they could hear the low murmur of reporters gathering, the occasional flash of a camera visible through the curtains. The world was waiting, but in the house, time seemed to stand still.

A sharp knock at the door made them both jump. Their lawyer, Veronica Steele, arrived with a purposeful stride, her high heels clicking authoritatively on the hardwood floor. Her briefcase was clutched like a shield, knuckles white against the leather. The scent of her crisp, no-nonsense perfume cut through the baby powder air, bringing a sense of the outside world they were about to face.

Veronica's presence filled the room with a fierce determination that was almost palpable. Her sharp eyes took in Mary's pallor and Ted's nervous fidgeting, softening slightly with understanding.

'Are you ready?' she asked.

Mary took a deep, shaky breath, smoothing down her skirt with clammy hands. She could hear the twins babbling in the next room, blissfully unaware of the day's significance. Their innocent sounds steeled her resolve.

'As ready as we'll ever be,' she replied, her voice stronger than she felt. Ted's hand found hers, squeezing tightly.

Veronica nodded, her posture straightening as if preparing for battle. 'Remember, you're not alone in this. we are going to see justice done for you and for your children.'

As they prepared to leave, Mary cast one last glance at the nursery. The soft, pastel colours and gentle mobile spinning lazily above the cots seemed a world away from the harsh reality of the courtroom they were about to face. With a deep breath, she stepped out into the unforgiving glare of camera flashes, clinging to Ted's hand like a lifeline.

. . .

The days ticking down to the trial had been extremely tense, and on numerous occasions, Mary had wanted to abandon the whole thing. She found herself caught between two worlds. One moment, they'd be discussing legal strategy; the next, changing nappies or soothing fussy babies. The juxtaposition was jarring, a constant reminder of the life they were fighting to protect.

The media presence outside their home had grown every day, transforming their quiet street into a circus. Reporters camped out, their cameras always at the ready. The simple act of leaving the house became an ordeal.

'We should say something,' Ted had mused one evening, peering through the blinds at the media scrum. 'Get our side of the story out there.'

Mary had shaken her head, her voice tired but resolute. 'No, Ted. You know what the lawyer said - we are the innocent parties; we don't have to say anything. This whole thing will be sorted in court, not on our road in front of our neighbours.'

Now, it was trial day and time to leave the safety and security of their home.

The imposing facade of the Old Bailey loomed before them, its weathered stone a reminder of the centuries of justice and judgment conducted in its walls. Mary and Ted stood at the foot of the steps, momentarily frozen by the gravity of what awaited them inside. The bustling streets of London seemed to fade away, leaving only the thundering of their hearts and the soft coos of the twins in their pram.

As they ascended the stairs, Mary's hand gripped the pram handle so tightly that her knuckles turned white. Each step felt like a mountain climbed, the weight of their ordeal threatening to pull them back down. The cool morning air carried the scent of damp stone and car exhaust.

Inside, the vaulted ceilings and echoing corridors of the courthouse swallowed them whole. Portraits of stern-faced judges looked down from the walls, their painted eyes seeming to follow the Browns as they made their way to the designated waiting area.

The hard wooden benches offered little comfort as they settled in next to Rosie and Edna, who were on hand to look after the twins. The ticking of a large clock on the wall marked the agonising passage of time, each second bringing them closer to the moment they'd face their child's kidnappers.

As they sat in the waiting room, the gravity of the situation seemed to press down on them. Mary bounced George on her knee, her eyes distant. Ted attempted to burp Daisy, his movements careful, as if his child might disappear at any moment.

The courtroom drama that unfolded over the next few days was intense and emotionally draining. Mary's testimony was a portrait of a mother's love and anguish, her words painting a vivid picture of their ordeal..

Ted's turn on the stand was equally powerful. He maintained his composure through most of his testimony, but when the defence attorney began to insinuate negligence on their part, his carefully controlled emotions broke through.

'Negligence?' he said, his voice tight with suppressed anger. 'What happened to us wasn't negligence. It was a deliberate act that tore our family apart. That robbed us of precious months with our daughter.'

Mary and Ted clung to each other for support as the trial progressed, drawing strength from their bond. The strain was evident in the tightness around their eyes and in the way they held themselves, always alert and watchful.

. . .

The moment Richard took the stand, the air in the courtroom seemed to thicken. Mary's breath caught in her throat, her heart pounding so loudly she was sure everyone could hear it. The man before her was both familiar and a stranger. His eyes darted nervously around the room.

As Richard began to speak, his voice trembling slightly, Mary felt a surge of emotions she couldn't quite name. Anger, certainly, but also a bewildering mix of pity and disgust. His words washed over her in waves, threatening to pull her under.

Mary noticed his mother in the gallery. Margaret Hartley's perfectly manicured fingers twisted a designer scarf with barely contained rage. Her lipstick—Chanel Rouge Allure—had strayed beyond perfect lines, suggesting crack in expensive façade. Her hair was like a helmet - styled and lacquered to within an inch of its life.

'I... I never meant for it to go this far,' Richard stammered, his hands fidgeting with his tie. 'Mary made me believe we had a future together. One date, and I saw our whole lives laid out before us. I couldn't let that go.'

The absurdity of his claim hit Mary like a physical blow. One date. One insignificant evening years ago, this man had woven an entire fantasy around it, a fantasy that had nearly destroyed her family. She could taste bile in the back of her throat, her nails digging crescents into her palms as she fought to maintain her composure.

Every fibre of Mary's being screamed to stand up, to shout at Richard, to make him understand the depth of pain and fear he had caused. The words bubbled up inside her, a torrent of rage and hurt begging for release. But she remained seated, her jaw clenched so tight it ached, Ted's hand in hers the only thing anchoring her to reality.

As Richard's testimony continued, Mary studied him, looking at the man who had upended her life. She saw the slight tremor in his hands, the way he seemed to shrink under the weight of his own words. And in that moment, Mary realised that Richard was just a man - a deeply flawed, delusional man whose actions had caused immeasurable harm, but a man nonetheless. He wasn't a monster in the shadows but a ridiculous man who deserved to be locked up. This realisation didn't lessen her anger or erase the trauma, but it allowed her to see the situation with a clarity she hadn't before. It made him feel like less of a threat.

During cross-examination break, Mary felt eyes burning into her back. She turned to find Margaret Hartley staring at her, elegant in Chanel suit that couldn't quite disguise rage's tremors. The older woman's perfectly manicured nails dug into leather handbag strap, knuckles white with tension.

'All her fault,' Margaret shouted, voice carrying in court-house quiet. 'Destroyed my children. My beautiful children.'

Officers moved in to remove the woman from the courtroom. Ted's hand found Mary's, squeezing gently. But she couldn't shake the image of Margaret's face—controlled fury beneath sophisticated veneer, lipstick bleeding slightly at corners like warning sign.

FINALLY, after what felt like an eternity, the jury reached their verdict. As the forewoman stood, Mary gripped Ted's hand so tightly her knuckles turned white.

'We, the jury, find the defendants... guilty on all counts.'

The courtroom erupted in a flurry of activity, but for Mary and Ted, the world seemed to slow down. They sat, hands clasped, experiencing a whirlwind of emotions. Relief, certainly. A sense of justice served. But also a lingering anxiety, a realisation that while the legal battle was over, the emotional scars remained.

That night, as they tucked the twins into their cots, Mary began to sing softly. It was the same lullaby she'd sung during those long, dark months of separation.

Daisy and George lay quietly, their eyes wide, little hands reaching out as if to grab hold of the music itself.

As the last notes faded away, Mary and Ted stood in the soft glow of the night light, arms around each other, watching their children drift off to sleep.

'We did it,' Mary whispered, her voice barely audible. 'We actually did it.'

Ted nodded, pulling her closer. 'We did. we are going to be okay, aren't we?'

FIRST STEPS, NEW BEGINNINGS

The day of the twins' first birthday arrived, and the living room had been transformed into a wonderland of soft colours and twinkling lights. Balloons bobbed gently against the ceiling, and streamers draped every surface, creating a cocoon of celebration.

Mary stood in the centre, cradling a twin in each arm, her eyes misty with emotion. 'Can you believe it?' she whispered to Ted. 'A year ago, we were... and now we are here.'

Ted wrapped his arms around his family, his chin resting on Mary's head. 'I know. It's like we are living in some beautiful dream.'

Right, no time to stand around; I need to put the finishing touches to my magnificent cake.'

'Is that the lump of mess on the kitchen counter?'

'What? That's a glorious cake.'

'Yeah, OK,' said Ted, nudging his wife affectionately.

The cake was meant to resemble the twins' favourite stuffed animals—a bear and a rabbit—but Ted was right—it looked like a pile of misshaped sponge. Hopefully, the vanilla and buttercream icing would bring it to life.

'Oh, Mary,' her mother's voice cut through her concentration. 'That looks dreadful. You should have said something. I could have bought one and brought it with me.'

Mary looked up, catching sight of her mother's barely concealed horror at the cake's appearance. She couldn't help but chuckle. 'It's fine, Mum. Honestly, I'm very happy with my abomination.'

'Mmmm... were you drunk when you made it?'

'No, I was not. It's not *that* bad.'

Before Rosie could comment further, the sound of the doorbell cut through the chatter, and Ted's warm, welcome voice carried from the hallway. 'Bob! Come in, come in. And is that Ricky I see behind you?'

Bob the Butcher, a mountain of a man with a heart to match, ducked through the doorway, his arms laden with gifts. A wide grin split his usually stern face. 'Couldn't miss the little ones' big day, could I? And look what I've brought!' He proudly held up two identical wooden rocking horses, their manes flowing and tails swishing.

Ricky from the antique shop followed close behind, his wiry frame contrasting Bob's bulk. He cradled an ornate music box in his hands, its gilt edges catching the light. 'It plays 'Twinkle, Twinkle, Little Star',' he explained, his eyes twinkling. 'Thought it might help with bedtime.'

As Mary emerged from the kitchen to greet them, a lump formed in her throat. These men and so many others had been instrumental in the search for Daisy. Their unwavering support and determination had been a lifeline during the darkest days.

Before she could speak, another knock at the door heralded the arrival of Andy and Dave from the café. They came bearing an enormous teddy bear between them, nearly as tall as Dave himself.

'We couldn't decide on just one gift,' Andy explained sheepishly.

'So we got them all,' Dave finished with a grin.

The house filled quickly after that, a steady stream of family and friends pouring in. The twins, wide-eyed with wonder, explored their newly decorated domain.

Just as Mary was about to suggest moving to the garden for cake, another knock came at the door. She opened it to find Detective Bronson standing on the threshold, flanked by two other officers. All three wore civilian clothes, looking slightly out of place amidst the festive atmosphere.

'I hope we are not intruding,' Bronson said, offering a small smile. In her arms, she held a gift-wrapped package. 'We just wanted to drop this off for the twins.'

Mary felt a complex swirl of emotions—gratitude, residual fear, relief—but she pushed it aside, welcoming them in with a warm smile. 'Of course, please come in. we are just about to cut the terrible cake I made,' she said. 'And I'm about to make a speech.'

As the chatter died down, Mary cleared her throat, suddenly nervous. 'I... we - Ted and I - want to thank you all for being here today. Not just for this celebration, but for everything you've done for us over the past year.'

Her gaze swept over the assembled crowd, lingering on each face. 'Bob, Ricky, Andy, Dave - you never gave up. Your posters, searches, and unwavering belief that we'd find Daisy meant more than we can ever express.'

She turned to the police officers. 'Detective Bronson, Officers Johnson and Patel - your dedication went above and beyond the call of duty. You became more than just investigators; you became our lifeline, our hope.'

Tears glistened in her eyes as she continued. 'To our families - Mum, Ted's parents, and yes, even you, Dad.' She offered a watery smile to her father, Derek, who had arrived late and stood slightly apart from the group. His recent separation from Rosie hung in the air, but today, it seemed insignificant in the face of all they had overcome.

'Your love and support carried us through the darkest days. And now, as we celebrate Daisy and George's birthday, we are not just marking another year. we are celebrating family, community, and the incredible strength of the human spirit.

As Mary finished speaking, a hush fell over the garden. Then, slowly, applause began to build, punctuated by sniffles and murmurs of agreement. Ted pulled her close, pressing a kiss to her temple.

Mary took a deep breath, her eyes scanning the faces of their loved ones.

'There's something else Ted and I would like to share with you all today,' she continued, her voice soft but clear. 'As grateful as we are for this home, which has been our sanctuary through so much, we've realised it's time for a change.'

She glanced at Ted, who nodded encouragingly. 'we are thinking of moving,' Mary announced, a mix of excitement and nostalgia colouring her words. 'As George and Daisy grow, we want them to have a playroom where their imaginations can run wild,' she said a soft smile on her lips. 'And as they get older, their own bedrooms.'

Ted stepped forward, placing his hand on the small of Mary's back in a gesture of support.

'It's a big step,' he added, his voice carrying across the garden. 'But after everything we've been through, we've learned the importance of creating a safe, happy environment for our family. This move feels like the next chapter in our story.'

Mary nodded, her eyes glistening. 'We wanted to share this with you all because you've been integral to our journey.

Your support has given us the strength and courage to look to the future with hope and excitement.'

She paused, her voice catching slightly. 'So while we celebrate Daisy and George's birthday today, we celebrate new beginnings. we are excited to start this new adventure and hope you'll all be a part of it.'

As she moved to cut the cake, Mary caught sight of her parents. They stood side by side, not touching but united in their love for their grandchildren. It wasn't perfect, but it was family in all its complicated, messy glory.

The afternoon passed in a blur of cake, presents, and laughter. As the sun began to set, casting long shadows across the garden, guests departed. Mary found herself by the gate, saying goodbye to Detective Bronson.

'Thank you,' she said softly. 'For everything you did for us. For them.'

As the last guest left and twilight settled over the house, Mary and Ted sat on the floor of the twins' room, surrounded by new toys and the remnants of wrapping paper. A comfortable silence settled over them, broken only by the soft breathing of the babies.

Ted reached out, taking Mary's hand in his, and they sat there, bathed in the soft glow of the nightlight. Mary felt a profound sense of peace wash over her. The road had been long and fraught with unimaginable challenges, but they had emerged stronger, surrounded by love and support.

Tomorrow would bring new adventures and new challenges. But for now, in this moment, all was right in their world. And that, Mary realised, was the greatest gift of all.

NEW HOUSE, NEW ADVENTURES

Mary stood on the lawn of her new home, surrounded by a sea of cardboard boxes and packing tape, and smiled to herself. This was bloody lovely. It was not quite as near all the boutiques and cafes as their apartment, but it worked better for their life now. It was a safe place with a much larger garden for children to play in and a bus stop outside that went straight to work.

She'd been made marketing director of the DIY and gardening centre, despite the ludicrous interview when she was pregnant, and enjoyed a tiny corner of an office in which she could dream up fantastical marketing plans. Most of her daily work consisted of trying to engage Keith in more and more wild and crazy plans.

'But this will get us in the papers.'

'I know, but where will we find a hot air balloon and a camel?'

'Don't worry about that - I'll source the necessary marketing tools, I just need your approval to go ahead.'

The answer that came back was usually a 'Not this time, Mary, but we do appreciate your creative thinking.'

So she went back to making signs for outside the store and updating the social media sites with pictures of begonias. One day, she'd crack it and persuade him to do something insane.

Mary held a twin in each arm as she stood before the new house, their little hands clutched at her shirt as they took in their new surroundings. She breathed deeply, the scent of freshly mown grass and new beginnings filling her lungs. 'Well,' she said softly, 'here we are. Our fresh start. A lovely house for us to play all sorts of games in.'

Ted walked passed, his arms laden with baby-proofing equipment, and nodded in agreement. 'Yep - we are going to have lots of fun here, aren't we little monsters?'

The process of settling in was a whirlwind of activity. Ted, fuelled by paternal instinct and perhaps one too many cups of coffee, meticulously baby-proofed every corner of the house. Mary followed in his wake, arranging furniture and unpacking boxes, pausing occasionally to rescue a curious twin from investigating an open moving box or attempting to scale a stack of pillows.

As evening approached, a gentle knock at the door signalled the arrival of their new neighbours.

They opened the door to find a small group of smiling faces, arms laden with welcoming wine and chocolates. Barbara, their next-door neighbour, stepped forward. 'Welcome to the neighbourhood! we are so delighted to have you here,' she said.

'Thank you, that's so kind. I'm Mary, this is Ted, and these are Daisy and George.'

The afternoon unfolded into an impromptu welcome party hosted in Barbara's garden. Mary watched the twins toddle through the grass, giggling as they discovered butterflies and dandelions.

'This is... nice,' she admitted to Ted, leaning into his side. 'Different, but nice.'

'Yes, it's very different, isn't it? Lots of young families and children everywhere.'

'I can't imagine how Juan or my other bonkers friends would react to this, but it's nice to be close to other families.'

Ted wrapped an arm around her shoulders, pressing a kiss to her temple.

As the work on the new house continued, the great nursery debate began. Mary and Ted stood in the empty room, surrounded by paint swatches and theme ideas, each advocating for their vision of the perfect space for their children.

'We need something calming,' Mary insisted, swinging a paint roller around recklessly as she spoke. 'A soothing environment for sleep and rest.'

Ted countered, his eyes alight with imagination. 'But think of the possibilities for adventure and learning! Jungles, rockets, underwater worlds!'

Their playful argument was interrupted by one of the twins toddling in, plopping down happily in the middle of the room and looking up at them with wide, curious eyes. The sight melted their hearts and broke the tension.

'How about a compromise?' Mary suggested, with laughter in her voice. 'A 'Peaceful Forest Adventure' theme. Calm colours with hidden adventures for them to discover as they grow.'

Ted's face lit up. 'I love it. The best of both worlds.'

Together, they created a nursery that was both a tranquil haven and a world of wonder. Soft, muted greens and blues covered the walls, while hand-painted trees hosted a menagerie of friendly animals. The ceiling transformed into a night sky with glow-in-the-dark stars that winked at the cribs below.

Their first night in the new house raised Mary's concerns. Strange noises echoed through the unfamiliar space, setting Mary and Ted on edge. They crept through darkened hallways, investigating creaks and groans, only to discover the normal settling sounds of their new home.

As they lay in bed, listening to the house's nocturnal symphony, giggles replaced their earlier tension. The stress of the move and the lingering anxiety from the past year seemed to melt away in the face of this shared moment of absurdity.

The next morning dawned bright and clear, perfect for the Brown family's first picnic in the garden. They spread a blanket on the grass, an array of snacks surrounding them. The twins explored their new domain with huge enthusiasm, alternating between chasing butterflies and examining blades of grass with intense concentration.

Mary and Ted watched their children's antics, a mixture of joy and that ever-present parental vigilance in their eyes. They marvelled at Daisy's attempts to communicate with a curious squirrel and Georges's determination to catalogue every pebble in his path. All was well…for now.

STRANGE GOINGS ON

Mary noticed the car first—an expensive German model, too pristine for casual parking. It appeared different times each day, never quite close enough to read the number plate.

One Tuesday morning, hurrying twins into garden, she caught movement behind tinted windows. Their eyes met briefly before the car pulled away. It was impossible to see who was in there. The tinted windows had stood as a barrier between them.

That evening, Mary mentioned it to Ted. 'Perhaps I imagined...'

'I'll call Bronson,' he said, already reaching for phone. 'Better paranoid than complacent.'

The car didn't return, but Mary felt watched. Small disturbances accumulated—garden gate slightly ajar, post scattered differently than morning delivery would cause, shadows glimpsed then gone.

MORE TROUBLE

The rhythm of normal life had begun to reassert itself. Mary found herself relaxing into motherhood's gentle patterns, fear's sharp edges slowly softening. Perhaps that's why she didn't immediately register the significance of small changes—a plant pot turned upside down in the garden, a fence panel missing.

Mary was too focused on handling the increasingly reckless duo. Daisy was the self-appointed adventurer of the duo, had taken the phrase 'climb every mountain' as a personal challenge. No surface was too high, no bookshelf too daunting for her to attempt to scale. Mary and Ted had become experts in the art of strategic furniture arrangement, turning their living room into a Tetris-like puzzle designed to thwart their pint-sized mountaineer.

'I swear,' Ted panted, having just performed an Olympic-worthy dive to catch Daisy as she attempted to summit Mount Refrigerator. 'She's part monkey, part human. I've never known anything like it. Do you think all little girls are like this?'

'Let's just be grateful she hasn't figured out how to open

the baby gates. I'm sure those things are the only reason we haven't woken up to find her on the roof.'

George had developed a passionate love affair with books that bordered on the obsessive. His idea of a wild time involved building precarious towers of literature and sitting in the middle of his paper-and-ink fortress, 'reading' with the intensity of a scholar deciphering ancient texts. The fact that most of his books were currently upside down and consisted primarily of pictures of farm animals did nothing to deter his scholarly pursuits.

'Moo,' he would declare solemnly, pointing to a particularly vibrant illustration of a chicken. 'Moo book.'

Ted, ever the supportive father, would nod sagely. 'Ah yes, the rare and elusive Moo Chicken. A fascinating species known for its ability to confuse farmers and defy the laws of nature. Excellent choice of reading material, son.'

As if the emerging personalities of their tiny terrors weren't enough to keep them on their toes, Mary and Ted found themselves embarking on the Herculean task of potty training. Their house became a minefield of portable potties, each one a monument to the ongoing battle between toddler bladders and parental sanity.

One particularly memorable afternoon found Ted attempting to coax Daisy into using the potty by performing what he called his 'Pee Pee Dance of Encouragement.' It was a spectacle that involved a lot of hip-wiggling, exaggerated facial expressions, and a catchy little ditty that went something like, 'Tinkle, tinkle, little star, how I wonder where you are? In the potty, not the floor, that's what big girl pants are for.'

Walking in on this performance, Mary paused in the doorway, her expression a perfect blend of amusement and embarrassment. 'You know,' she said, trying desperately to keep a straight face, 'when we decided to have kids, I don't recall 'interpretive toilet-themed dance routines' being in the job description.'

Ted, mid-shimmy, grinned unabashedly. 'Hey, whatever works, right?'

Just as it seemed Ted's unique approach might be working, with Daisy giggling and approaching the potty, disaster struck. In his enthusiasm, Ted executed a particularly vigorous spin, lost his footing and went down in a flailing heap of limbs and misplaced confidence.

What happened next could only be described as a perfect storm of slapstick comedy and questionable physics. Ted's fall created a domino effect, sending nearby toys, books, and the potty flying.

For a moment, there was stunned silence. Then Daisy, delighted by this unexpected turn of events, clapped her hands and declared, 'Again. Daddy slide.'

THE TWINS' vocabulary exploded like linguistic fireworks, and family dinners became an exercise in improvisational comedy. Words were mangled, meanings were muddled, and Mary and Ted played an ongoing game of 'Guess What the Toddler Meant.'

One memorable evening, as they sat around the dinner table, George pointed excitedly at his plate and declared, 'Spooky noodles.'

'Spooky noodles?' Ted repeated, peering at the plate of perfectly ordinary spaghetti. 'Should we be concerned that our pasta has joined the ranks of the undead?'

Mary, ever the translator, shook her head. 'I think he means 'spaghetti.'

Not to be outdone, Daisy chimed in with her linguistic masterpiece. Pointing at Ted, she announced proudly, 'Daddy hairy face.'

Ted's hand flew to his chin, where a few days' worth of stubble had accumulated. 'Hairy face monster?' he gasped in mock outrage. 'I'll have you know this is a very distinguished beard-in-progress. I'm going for the rugged look.'

Mary snorted. 'More like the I-forgot-where-we-keep-the-razors look. But don't worry, honey. You make a very handsome hairy-face monster.'

As the year progressed, the twins' unique vocabulary turned dinner into a linguistic scavenger hunt. Forks became 'food stabbies,' milk was 'moo juice,' and broccoli was dubbed 'tiny trees' (though this last one was Ted's contribution in a valiant but futile attempt to make vegetables more appealing).

Mary and Ted were in stitches by the end of every meal, their sides aching from laughter. 'You know,' Mary said, wiping tears of joy from her eyes, 'we should write a dictionary. 'The Toddler's Guide to Mangling the English Language: A Brown Family Production.''

Ted nodded enthusiastically. 'That's exactly what I'm going to do. Now, are you sure you're going to be OK if I pop out for a while? Just to meet up with some of the guys for a couple of pints?'

'Of course. Do you want me to drop you off?'

'No. Don't be daft. You stay here. I'll only be a couple of hours.'

THE TWINS' soft breathing through the baby monitor provided counterpoint to Mary's footsteps on the stairs. It was only 9pm. She'd retired early but couldn't sleep, so was heading downstairs in search of ice cream. Half way down the stairs she heard a sound. A scrape against linoleum, too deliberate for house settling.

Her fingers found her phone, muscle memory selecting

Ted's number. The kitchen tap dripped its steady rhythm while she waited, each drop echoing impossibly loud.

'Ted?' Her whisper caught in her throat. Blood rushed in her ears as another sound emerged from below—a drawer sliding open, cutlery rattling.

'Mary? What's wrong?'

'Someone's in the house. Downstairs. I can hear—'

A cupboard door clicked shut.

'Oh God.'

'Get to the twins. Now. I'm coming. Call the police.'

She terminated Ted's call, fingers trembling as she pressed 999. The dispatcher's voice carried practiced calm: 'Police, fire, or ambulance?'

'Police. Please. Someone's in my house. 47 Sycamore Lane. I have two babies upstairs...'

Kitchen light spilled suddenly into the hallway. Mary pressed herself against the wall, heart hammering so hard she feared it might give her away. A shadow moved across the illuminated patch of carpet at the stairs' base.

The back door's familiar squeal cut through darkness. Then silence, broken only by her own ragged breathing.

The sound of sirens could he heard as the door flew open and Ted ran in.

'Where is he?' Ted screamed.

'I don't know. I think he's gone,' said Mary.

Ted ran up to his wife and held her while she cried on his shoulder.

Torchlight preceded uniformed officers through her front door minutes later. They found her still frozen on the stairs, phone clutched like talisman, her husband beside her, looking furious.

'Clear downstairs,' one called.

Mary followed them into her kitchen.

Three words defaced her mirror, red lipstick dripping like blood: I HATE YOU.

'Jesus,' Ted breathed, pulling her close. The scent of his familiar aftershave mingled with evening air flowing through the still-open back door.

PRE-SCHOOL

In the days and weeks after the break-in, security measures transformed their home into fortress—cameras, sensors, upgraded locks.

They did everything they could to make their home as safe as possible without terrifying their children. Daisy and George were old enough to sense that something was going on, as police officers dusted for prints, and workmen came and went.

Mary tried hard not to let fear imprison them. They would make their house as safe as possible and allow the police to do their work.

Each morning brought small victories: first smile, new word, moment of perfect peace. They would not surrender joy to shadows.

As the twins grew and their personalities blossomed, Mary and Ted faced a new challenge: preschool. The search for the perfect educational environment became an odyssey, with each school tour revealing new pros, cons, and occasionally, reasons to question the sanity of early childhood educators everywhere.

'I don't know, Ted,' Mary whispered as they left the third school of the day, a place that seemed to think macaroni art was the pinnacle of educational achievement. 'Do you think we are being too picky?'

'I don't know. As long as they are safe and well looked-after I don't really care. I don't want them to be at any risk at all though.'

'Of course.'

'Big gates.'

'Sure.'

'With padlocks.'

'Yep.'

'And lions patrolling outside.'

'That might be harder to find.'

'A moat of snakes.'

'Again - quite hard to guarantee that we'll find a school with that.'

IT WASN'T until they were discussing their options over dinner (or rather, over the remains of dinner, as most of it seemed to have ended up on the floor, the walls, and somehow, the ceiling) that the real challenge became apparent.

'The schools need to be right for their personalities,' Mary said. 'There's no such thing as good schools and bad schools - it's all about what's right for them.'

'Wait a minute,' Ted said, a forkful of what might have once been creamy chicken hovering halfway to his mouth. 'If we choose different schools based on their personalities, does that mean we'd be separating them?'

The thought hit Mary like a ton of brightly coloured building blocks. 'Oh,' she breathed, the implications sinking in. 'I hadn't even considered... do you think they're ready for that? Are we ready for that?'

They looked over at the twins, who were currently engaged in what appeared to be a very serious conversation about the merits of various dinosaurs (though given their limited vocabulary, it sounded more like 'Rawr' 'Stomp stomp').

'Maybe we are overthinking this,' Ted suggested, watching as George solemnly offered Daisy half of his cookie, a gesture of sibling love if ever there was one. 'They're individuals, sure, but they're also a team. Maybe we should look for a place that can nurture both aspects.'

Mary nodded slowly, feeling some of the tension ease from her shoulders. 'You're right. We'll find a place that's right for both of them. Together.'

Evening found them arranged in unconscious tableau—Ted surrounded by sleeping children, prehistoric literature abandoned mid-narrative. Mary's heart constricted at the sight, love's familiar ache intensified by memory of what they'd nearly lost.

Carefully so as not to disturb the sleeping trio, she tiptoed into the room. She gently removed the book from Ted's lap, marking his place (though she had a feeling they'd be revisiting the thrilling world of underwear-less dinosaurs many times in the near future). Then, pressing a soft kiss to each forehead—Ted's, Daisy's, and George's—she whispered, 'I love you, my little family. More than you'll ever know.'

As she turned to leave, Ted's eyes fluttered open briefly. 'Hey,' he mumbled, his voice thick with sleep. 'Did I miss the part where the T-Rex tries on a thong?'

Mary stifled a laugh. 'Go back to sleep, you goof. We can explore the fascinating world of dinosaur undergarments tomorrow.'

Ted nodded sleepily, his eyes already drifting shut again. 'Love you.'

'Love you too,' Mary whispered, her heart full to bursting.

As she quietly closed the nursery door behind her, Mary leaned against the wall, taking a moment to process her overwhelming love and gratitude.

The terrible twos, with all their tantrums and trials, had also brought tremendous joy. Every new word, every milestone, every tiny victory was a reminder of how far they'd come and how much they had to be thankful for.

There had been no more attempts to break in to their home, and the police had been great at driving past at regular intervals, and staying in contact with them.

Making her way to the living room, Mary began to tidy up the day's chaos - stacking books, corralling runaway toys, and rescuing Ted's ties from their new life as superhero capes. As she worked, she hummed softly, the same lullaby she'd sung to the twins when they were babies when Daisy was missing and every night since their return.

The simple act of straightening up became a meditation of sorts, each item a tangible reminder of their life together: the sippy cup with the stubborn lid that had led to Ted's impromptu juggling act at breakfast, the half-finished puzzle that had kept George occupied for hours, his little face scrunched in concentration, and the glitter-covered art project that Daisy had proudly declared was a 'sparkly dinosaur-princess-rocket ship.'

By the time she finished, the living room looked less like the aftermath of a toddler tornado and more like a lived-in, love-filled family home. Mary sank onto the sofa, surrounded by the evidence of their wonderfully chaotic life, and felt a sense of peace settle over her.

She curled up on the couch, pulling a throw blanket over herself (one that had clearly been used as a cape, a picnic blanket, and possibly a parachute in some elaborate toddler scheme), and she closed her eyes.

As the Brown household settled into the quiet of night, the only sounds were the soft snores from the nursery and the occasional creak of the house settling.

THE BREAK-IN

It was the sound of breaking glass that alerted Mary to the break-in.

Ted was still asleep in the twins room, having nodded off while reading a bedtime story. Mary lay still. Why wasn't the alarm going off?

There was silence downstairs. Perhaps she had imagined it.

She lay her head on the pillow, listening intently. Then she heard kitchen sounds—a drawer sliding open, objects being moved. Someone muttering.

She was too terrified to get out of bed, so reached for her phone on the bedside table and rang Ted. His phone went straight to answerphone. Shit.

Nine-nine-nine. Each number pressed with fierce concentration.

'Emergency services, which service do you require?'

'Police.' Her whisper emerged surprisingly steady. 'Someone's broken into forty-seven Sycamore Lane. I have twins. The person's coming up the stairs—'

As if summoned by her words, creaking wood announced

slow ascent. Each step punctuated by pause, like the intruder was gathering courage.

'Units are four minutes away,' the dispatcher murmured. 'Stay on the line. Find somewhere safe—'

'No.' Mary surprised herself with the steel in her whisper. 'I'm not hiding. Not in my own home. Not again.' She positioned herself in the doorway, phone pressed to ear like lifeline. As soon as the guy opened the door she would lash out.

The landing light clicked on. Shadow movements visible beneath door.

Mary's heart thundered against ribs as the door handle turned with excruciating slowness. She could hear ragged breathing from the other side.

'The police are nearly here,' she shouted. 'Leave now.'

The door swung inward.

Margaret Hartley stood illuminated by landing light, smaller than memory painted her. Designer coat hung loose on diminished frame, grey hair unkempt. Her hand trembled against doorframe.

'They were good children,' she whispered. Chanel Rouge Allure lipstick smeared at corners of her mouth. 'Such good children before you ruined everything.'

Blue lights strobed through curtains, painting walls in electric midnight. Siren wail crescendoed.

The door to the twins room opened and Ted came charging out.

'My Richard...' Mrs. Hartley's voice cracked. 'My beautiful boy...'

'Your beautiful boy helped steal my baby.' Mary's words emerged glacial. 'Your daughters took my child.'

Ted approached her from behind, grabbing her in a hold around her neck. 'How dare you come into my house. How dare you.'

There was the sound of crashing wood as the police came

through the door. Boots thundered up stairs. Mrs. Hartley's shoulders slumped as officers appeared behind her, Detective Bronson's familiar figure among them.

'I am arresting you for breaking and entering. You do not have to say anything. But, it may harm your defence if you do not mention when questioned something which you later rely on in court. Anything you do say may be given in evidence.'

Dawn painted sky pink beyond nursery windows. In distance, a police car door slammed. Margaret Hartley's designer heels clicked down path one final time, handcuffs glinting in growing light.

AN UPDATE FROM BRONSON

Mary and Ted collapsed onto the sofa, relieved to have got through another horror, but worn out with the stress of it all. The only good news in all this was that the twins had slept through everything.

They watched, in silence, as officers dusted for finger prints and took photographs.

'You have a hell of a security system here,' said one of the men. 'You've just got to remember to switch it on.'

'Yes,' said Mary, sheepishly.

There's no doubt that their new security system had transformed the house into something approaching a fortress—CCTV covering every approach, motion sensors guarding windows, sophisticated alarms that could detect even subtle changes in air pressure when doors opened.

But it had been Ted who managed the nightly routine with military precision: checking monitors, activating sensors, setting the multi-point alarm.

With Ted falling asleep with the twins, it had fallen to Mary to switch everything on. And she'd completely forgotten. The system's control panel downstairs displayed its dormant blue light instead of the steady green that indicated active protection.

It was this small oversight—born of altered routine—that had provided Margaret Hartley her opportunity.

Now that the woman had been arrested, though, the final thread of the nightmare had unravelled. Over the next few days, Mary felt tension release like a physical weight lifting. Perhaps now, finally, they could truly begin healing. Ted's suggestion of a birthday party at the house and a seaside holiday carried the promise of a fresh start.

The Browns decided to make the party a celebration for all the local children. The garden was transformed into a whimsical wonderland for the occasion. Streamers danced in the gentle breeze, their vibrant colours in stark contrast against the clear azure sky. Balloons in every hue of the rainbow bobbed cheerfully, tethered to chairs and fences, their glossy surfaces reflecting the warm sunlight. At the centre of it all stood a cake that was a masterpiece of confectionery art, its three candles waiting patiently to be lit.

Mary surveyed the scene with a mixture of pride and quiet amazement. The journey from those dark days of separation to this moment of celebration felt both impossibly long and startlingly brief. She watched as tiny humans darted about the yard, their laughter a melody that seemed to make the very air shimmer with happiness.

In one corner, a group of children were engaged in a game that defied easy categorisation. It seemed to involve a great deal of running, spinning, and spontaneous bouts of what could only be described as interpretive dance. Mary found herself mesmerised by their uninhibited joy, their movements a physical manifestation of the pure, uncomplicated happiness that only children seem capable of achieving.

Nearby, Ted was orchestrating a game of pin-the-tail-on-the-dinosaur with all the gravity of a conductor leading a symphony orchestra. His face was a study in concentration as he carefully blindfolded each child, gently spun them around, and pointed them in the general direction of the poster. The results were entertainingly haphazard, with tails ending up in some truly creative places.

'Remember, aim for the big green thing,' Ted was saying to a little girl whose blindfold had slipped just enough for her to peek out. Her mischievous grin suggested she had plans that didn't necessarily align with Ted's instructions. 'That's right, the dinosaur. Not me, not the trees, and definitely not Mr Whiskers.'

The aforementioned Mr Whiskers, the Browns' new cat, had taken refuge under a nearby bush, his tail twitching in a manner that suggested he was reconsidering his life choices.

Mary felt a smile tug at her lips as she watched Ted navigate the chaotic waters of children's party games. Three years ago, the idea of hosting a birthday party for the twins had seemed like an impossible dream. Now, here they were, surrounded by friends, family, and enough sugar to fuel a small country for a week.

As if summoned by her thoughts, Daisy and George came racing across the yard, their faces flushed with excitement and smeared with what Mary hoped was chocolate but suspected might be a creative mixture of cake frosting and garden soil.

'Mummy! Mummy!' Daisy called out, her voice pitched high with excitement. She skidded to a stop in front of Mary, her copper curls bouncing wildly around her face. 'Can we open presents now? Pretty please with a cherry and a unicorn and a rocket ship on top?'

George, not to be outdone, added his own plea. 'Yeah, and

can we eat the cake? I promise I'll use a fork this time, not my hands.'

Mary crouched down, bringing herself to eye level with her little tornados. She took in their bright eyes, flushed cheeks, and the unmistakable air of barely contained excitement that surrounded them like an aura.

'Not just yet, my loves,' she said, her voice gentle but firm. 'we are still waiting for a couple of special guests. But how about you go help Daddy with his dinosaur game? I think he could use some expert palaeontologists.'

The twins' eyes lit up at the prospect of 'helping', and they zoomed off towards Ted, who looked delighted and apprehensive at their approach. Mary watched them go, marvelling at their boundless energy and the way they seemed to light up every corner of the yard they passed through.

Just as Mary was contemplating the logistics of wrangling two dozen sugar-fuelled reception children for cake time, a familiar voice caught her attention.

'Well, well, if it isn't the birthday girl herself. Looking much less sleep-deprived than the last time I saw you, I must say.'

Mary turned to see Detective Bronson standing at the gate, a wrapped gift under one arm and an expression that suggested she was both pleased and slightly out of her element at a children's birthday party. The detective's usual stern demeanour had softened somewhat, though she still carried herself with the alert posture of someone more accustomed to crime scenes than cake ceremonies.

'Detective Bronson,' Mary exclaimed, genuine warmth infusing her voice. 'I'm so glad you could make it. Please, come in. Fair warning, though - enter at your own risk. We've got a high concentration of reception children fuelled by juice boxes and the promise of cake. It's like a very small, very sticky United Nations.'

Bronson chuckled, stepping into the yard. Her eyes scanned the scene with the habitual thoroughness of a law enforcement officer, though her gaze softened as it landed on the children playing. 'I've faced down hardened criminals and navigated crime scenes. Surely I can handle a few pint-sized party-goers.'

No sooner had the words left her mouth than a small figure in a princess costume darted past, narrowly avoiding a collision with the detective's legs. The little girl paused for a moment, looking up at Bronson with wide, curious eyes.

'This is Detective Bronson, she's a police officer,' Mary said.

'Wow. Are you a real police officer?' asked the little girl, her voice filled with awe. 'Do you catch bad guys?'

Bronson, caught off guard by the direct question, nodded. 'Yes, I am. And yes, sometimes I do catch bad guys.'

The little girl's face lit up with excitement. 'Cool! I want to be a police officer too. Or maybe a unicorn.'

With that declaration, she was off again, leaving a slightly bemused Bronson in her wake.

Mary laughed at the expression on the detective's face. 'Welcome to the wonderful world of four-year-old logic. Where being a unicorn and a police officer are equally viable career options.'

As the party progressed, Mary found herself drawing Bronson aside for a quieter conversation. 'What's the latest information on Mrs Hartley?' she asked.

Bronson shifted into professional mode. 'As you're aware, the Crown Prosecution Service has fast-tracked the case. Breaking and entering, criminal damage, harassment causing fear of violence—they're pursuing all charges.'

'How long is she likely to get?' Mary kept her voice low, conscious of nearby parents.

'After the first hearing yesterday at magistrates' court,

things aren't looking promising for her,' Bronson replied. 'She was shouting out, much as she did at Richard's trial. Given the severity and her previous behaviour, they've remanded her in custody. No bail.'

Mary exhaled slowly. 'I'd heard she was denied bail. I didn't realise about the outbursts, though.'

'Indeed. It wasn't a particularly dignified performance. Previous incidents worked against her as well: two break-ins, documented psychiatric concerns,' Bronson's tone held professional satisfaction. 'Crown Court date's set for three weeks' time. Should be straightforward—we have DNA from both scenes, CCTV footage, witness statements.'

'And until then?'

'She's in Bronzefield—women's prison in Surrey. Good security, proper psychiatric support.' Bronson watched Daisy toddle past clutching a balloon. 'You can properly relax now, Mary. Take that holiday Ted's been planning.'

'Does that mean she'll get the maximum sentence?'

'Given the circumstances—targeting a family with young children, previous warning, psychological impact given your history—CPS is pushing for five years. She'll serve at least half that in custody, rest on licence with strict conditions including a restraining order.'

Mary nodded, watching Ted organise an impromptu game of musical statues. 'Sometimes I feel guilty. Three children in prison, now their mother...'

'They made their choices,' Bronson said firmly. 'All you did was survive their actions and protect your family.'

A cheer went up as George won musical statues, his serious face breaking into a delighted grin.

'Right then,' Bronson said, setting down her cup. 'I'd better head off. Court updates will come through victim support, but call me if you need anything.'

'Thank you,' Mary said quietly. 'For everything.' She paused before adding, 'Will you be at the trial?'

'I'll be there. Will you and Ted attend?'

'Ted will definitely go,' Mary said. 'I don't know whether I can face any more courtrooms. Unless I'm required to give evidence?'

'No need,' Bronson assured her. 'Given the straightforward nature of the break-ins and the existing restraining order, your written victim impact statement will suffice. CPS considers the physical evidence compelling enough—DNA, CCTV footage, forensics from both scenes.'

'What about Ted's statement?'

'His written statement covers the impact on family life, security measures you've had to implement, psychological effect on you all. Very compelling material.'

Mary sank into a garden chair with visible relief. 'I wasn't looking forward to seeing her again.'

'Understandable. The prosecution has medical reports, psychiatric evaluations, and documentation of her escalating behaviour. Plus testimony from the officers who arrested her both times. Your previous case history with the family adds significant weight.'

'And the restraining order?'

'Will be extended to lifetime prohibition once she's convicted. No contact, no approaching within five miles of your home, workplace, or the children's future schools. Any violation means immediate recall to prison.'

'When will we know?'

'Trial's set for the fifteenth. Given the evidence, should be wrapped up in two days. I'll let you know the outcome immediately.'

Mary heard her twins laughing in the garden with Ted. 'Thank you, Sarah. For everything.'

'Just doing my job,' Bronson paused. 'Though I must admit, this one's been personal. Take care, Mary. Enjoy that beach holiday—you've earned it.'

FULL CIRCLE

〜

'Come on, let's stop talking about the case,' said Bronson. 'Tell me about your beautiful children.'

Mary shared stories of the twins' early days and reflecting on how far they'd come. The initial tension of hosting a party had given way to a sense of grateful celebration.

'...and then,' Mary was saying, her eyes twinkling with mirth, 'Ted walks in, looking like he'd just gone ten rounds with a bag of flour. He looks at me, dead serious, and says, 'I think we need to revisit our nappy-changing strategy.' I don't think I've ever laughed so hard in my life.'

The women gathered around Mary chuckled appreciatively, their laughter blending with the joyful shrieks of children playing nearby. It created a symphony of happiness that seemed to hang in the air like a tangible thing.

Meanwhile, Ted found himself engrossed in conversation with another of the police officers who'd been instrumental during that painfully difficult time. They were reliving some of the more unusual moments of the investigation, finding humour in situations that had seemed anything but funny at the time.

'Remember that lead we got about the suspicious van?' Officer Johnson was saying, a smile playing at the corners of his mouth. 'Turned out to be a mobile pet grooming service. I've never seen so many confused poodles in my life.'

Ted nodded, chuckling. 'Oh yeah, what about when we thought we'd found a secret hideout, but it was just an elaborate treehouse? I still can't believe you climbed up in full tactical gear.'

Johnson shrugged, a twinkle in his eye. 'Hey, you never know. Could have been a very short, crafty kidnapper with a penchant for tree climbing.'

As the adults reminisced, the show's real stars were blissfully unaware of the significance of their guests. Daisy and George, surrounded by a mountain of colourfully wrapped presents, were in gift-opening heaven. Their faces shone with delight as they tore into package after package, each new reveal eliciting gasps of joy and excitement.

'Look, Mummy,' George exclaimed, holding up a toy detective kit with magnifying glass and notepad. His eyes were wide with wonder as he examined each item in turn. 'I can be just like the policeman in your stories!'

Not to be outdone, Daisy was already halfway into her new doctor's coat, the too-large garment hanging comically on her small frame. The stethoscope dangled around her neck, nearly reaching her knees. 'And I can be a doctor,' she declared proudly. 'I'll make everyone better, just like in your book, Mummy!'

Mary and Ted exchanged knowing glances, marvelling at the synchronicity of it all. Here were their children, unknowingly playing out roles that had been so crucial in their own story. It was a moment of perfect circularity, a reminder of how far they'd come and how beautifully life had a way of weaving past and present together.

As the party began to wind down, with sugar crashes

imminent and several children looking dangerously close to nap time meltdowns, a sense of peaceful contentment settled over the Brown backyard. The chaos of the day gave way to quieter moments, snapshots of joy that Mary knew she'd treasure forever.

The late afternoon sun cast a golden glow over the scene, turning everything it touched into a tableau of warmth and happiness. Mary watched as Daisy and George, their energy finally beginning to flag, curled up on a picnic blanket, surrounded by their new toys. Their heads were close together as they examined a picture book, their voices a soft murmur of shared wonder.

Ted approached, slipping an arm around Mary's waist. She leaned into him, drawing comfort from his solid presence. 'We did it,' he said softly, his voice filled with pride and awe. 'We made it through the terrible twos. Our kids are happy, healthy, and surrounded by love. It's more than I ever dared to hope for during those dark days.'

Mary nodded, feeling a lump form in her throat. 'It's everything I dreamed of and more,' she whispered. 'Look at them, Ted. They're so full of life, so curious about the world. And to think, we almost lost this.'

Ted tightened his arm around her, pressing a kiss to her temple. 'But we didn't,' he reminded her gently. 'We fought, we persevered, and we won. And now we get to enjoy moments like this.'

Daisy looked up from her book as if on cue, catching sight of her parents. Her face lit up with a smile of pure joy, and she waved enthusiastically. 'Mummy! Daddy! Come see! George found a picture of a dinosaur that looks just like the cake!'

Mary and Ted exchanged a glance, sharing a moment of silent communication. Then, hand in hand, they crossed the garden to join their children. As they settled onto the blanket, the twins began chattering excitedly about their discovery, their words tumbling over each other in their eagerness to share.

Watching her family, whole and happy together, Mary felt a sense of completion. They had come full circle, from the depths of despair to the heights of joy. The road had been long and often difficult, but every step had led them here to this moment of perfect happiness.

THE BIRTHDAY PARTY, with all its chaos and joy, moments of reflection and laughter, had been more than just a celebration of Daisy and George turning four. It had been a celebration of family, resilience, and the enduring power of love. As Mary looked around at the remnants of the day—deflating balloons, scattered wrapping paper, and the happy, tired faces of her loved ones—she felt a profound sense of gratitude.

This, she thought, was what happily ever after really looked like—not a static, perfect ending but a series of beautiful, messy, joy-filled moments strung together by love and shared experiences. As she helped Ted gather up sleepy twins and leftover cake, Mary knew that she wouldn't have it any other way.

Unimaginable challenges and incredible triumphs marked the Brown family's extraordinary journey. But as they closed the chapter on this milestone birthday, Mary realised that the most extraordinary thing was the everyday love that filled their lives. It was in the sticky kisses, the bedtime stories, the scraped knees and the burst of laughter. It was in the quiet and chaotic moments, in the tears and triumphs.

As they said goodbye to the last of their guests, the backyard now quiet save for the gentle rustling of leaves in the evening breeze, Mary felt a sense of peace settle over her. They had come full circle indeed, but this was not an ending. It was the beginning - of new adventures, challenges, and joys.

With a contented sigh, Mary turned to help Ted carry their sleeping children into the house. Tomorrow would bring new adventures, but for now, she was content to bask in the afterglow of a perfect day, surrounded by the love of her family.

THE FIRST HOLIDAY

Mary patted the sand on her newly-created castle, and looked at her children. She was full of pride at her magnificent creation.

'No,' repeated Daisy and George. 'No, mummy.'

'Ted - I'm being heckled by 2-year-olds.'

She gently threw the children onto the sand, tickling them and blowing raspberries on their tummies enjoying the screams of delight from her favourite two people in the world.

'Ted, Ted, come here,' Mary said, digging into the sand. 'There's something here.'

Ted rushed to her side.

'Are you OK? What have you found?'

'I think it might be a purse.'

'Ha, ha, ha…' said Ted, dropping onto the sand beside her. Someone must be feeling herself again if she's got her sense of humour back.'

'That was a mad honeymoon, though, wasn't it?' said Mary. 'Going off to St Lucia to enjoy a relaxing time on the beach with cocktails, and finding ourselves in the middle of a 'missing persons' investigation.'

'It was crackers,' said Ted. 'Why do these things always happen to us?'

'You know, I'm not sure. My whole life has been filled with crazy occurrences and daft adventures.'

'Like the safari?'

'Like the safari when I got stuck up a tree wearing nothing but my knickers.'

'Or that cruise you went on?'

'Yes, that was certainly bizarre - I went yomping through Europe with an old man.'

'And don't forget that mysterious invitation that turned up.'

'Top the funeral of someone I didn't know... yes, how could I forget.'

'It's all been fun though, hasn't it?'

'Oh God yes. I don't think I'd cope well with a normal life.'

'No, me neither.'

'Hopefully, things will be calmer now we have the children. I'm hoping the adventures will calm down and things will be calmer.'

'Yeah,' said Ted. 'I'm just not convinced that's going to happen.'

'Come here,' she said, pulling him down onto the sand next to her.

'Shall we tickle Daddy?' she said to the children. 'Shall we tickle Daddy so much that he cries?'

Daisy and George leapt onto their father, covering him with tickles and sandy kisses, clambering all over him and laughing in delight.

Ted responded by laughing as they tickled him, leading the children to greater levels of joy and excitement.

'Right then, troops,' Ted announced, his voice carrying the forced bravado of a man about to lead an expedition into uncharted territory. 'Let's set up base camp and watch everyone from behind our beach umbrella and blanket tent.'

'Yay,' shouted the kids, jumping in the sand in delight at all the fun.

As their beach day ended, the Brown family trudged back to their little cottage, tired, sandy, and slightly pinker than when they'd arrived. But their faces were split with smiles, the bone-deep happiness that comes from a day of simple pleasures and family togetherness.

Mary paused momentarily as they approached their cottage, taking in the scene. Ted, sensing her mood, stopped beside her.

'What is it, love?' he asked gently.

Mary shook her head, feeling a swell of emotion rise in her chest. 'It's just... I don't know, Ted. I've never felt more happy or contented. I think I realise what real happiness is for the first time.'

Ted shifted George to one arm, wrapping the other around Mary's shoulders. 'we are living the dream, sand in our shoes and all.'

As they stood there, their sleeping children in their arms and the sound of the ocean in their ears, Mary felt a profound sense of gratitude wash over her. With all its laughter, minor panics, and simple joys, this day was more than just a beach trip. It was a celebration of their family, of the bond that had seen them through the darkest of times and now allowed them to bask in the light of days like these.

'Come on,' Ted said after a moment, kissing Mary's temple. 'Let's get these little sand monsters inside and hosed off. I think we've all earned a good night's sleep.'

As they walked the final few steps to their cottage, sand crunching beneath their feet, Mary knew this day would live long in their memory. It was the day they truly began to heal, to laugh freely again, and to embrace the chaotic, beautiful mess that was their life together.

George and Daisy might not remember this day when they were older, but Mary knew she and Ted would never forget. It was the day they rediscovered the simple joy of being a family and realised they were surviving and thriving. And as she helped Ted hose the sand off their still-sleeping children, Mary couldn't help but look forward to all the adventures yet to come.

Life, they had discovered, offered its own peculiar poetry. Their happiness revealed itself not in perfect moments but in imperfect ones made perfect by love's presence.

ENDS

THERE'S A NEW SERIES ON THE SHELVES & IT'S FUNNIER THAN EVER!!

It's all about Rosie Brown, Mary's mum, and what she gets up to when she finds herself aged 60, single and ready to mingle. She joins up with other feisty 60-somethings and they have the time of their lives,

The series is four books long. This is the link to the first one:

UK: My Book

US: My Book

THE SASSY SIXTIES CLUB:

Get ready for a wild ride with Rosie Brown, the sassy

sixty-something determined to show the world that age is just a number.

Her mission to take control of her life begins when she gets out of bed and realises that every part of her is starting to creak. All she's done is lie down for eight hours, but she has the sort of neck pain that a younger person would associate with severe whiplash from a multi-car pile-up.

There are so many clicks and clacks from her creaking joints it sounds like someone's knitting next to her as she walks. Serenaded by knitting needles when she used to be serenaded by handsome young men. How on earth did this happen?

She catches her reflection and gasps - when did she start looking like her own grandmother? But hold onto your dentures, folks, because Rosie's not going down without a fight!

On the brink of divorce, disillusioned, and desperately eyeing those comfy Clarks shoes, Rosie decides it's time to dust off her leopard print and channel her inner twenty-something.

What follows is a hilarious journey of self-rediscovery that'll have you laughing, crying, and cheering from the sidelines.

Watch Rosie trade her sensible slacks for sassy stilettos as she shimmies through dance classes, leaving a trail of shocked faces and dropped jaws in her wake. Will her ex-husband Derek's eyes pop out of his head when he sees the new Rosie? You bet your bingo wings they will!

But the real fun begins when Rosie meets her new partners in crime - a gang of sixty-something troublemakers who prove that mischief has no age limit. From crashing singles mixers to staging senior citizen flash mobs, these golden girls are painting the town red... and maybe a few other colours they can't quite remember the names of.

Will Rosie find love again? Will she rediscover her zest for life? Or will she end up in a mobility scooter drag race down Main Street?

'Sassy and Sixty' is a heartwarming tale that proves it's never too late to rewrite your story - even if you need reading glasses to see the page.

So grab your most outrageous hat, pour yourself a cheeky glass of sherry, and get ready to join Rosie on the adventure of a lifetime!

Warning: This book may cause spontaneous laughter, uncontrollable urges to tango, and a sudden desire to dazzle your walking stick. Reader discretion is advised!

ALSO BY BERNICE BLOOM

The order of the Mary Brown books:

What's Up, Mary Brown? (The Mary Brown novels Book 1)

Link: **My Book**

The Adventures of Mary Brown (The Mary Brown novels Book 2)

Link: **My Book**

Christmas with Mary Brown: Fun, Joy & Laughter (The Mary Brown novels Book 3)

Link: **My Book**

Mary Brown is leaving town: Fun and laughter at weight loss camp & the joys of internet dating (The Mary Brown novels Book 4)

Link: **My Book**

Mary Brown in Lockdown (The Mary Brown novels Book 5)

Link: **My Book**

The Mysterious Invitation: A Mary Brown novel (The Mary Brown novels Book 6)

Link: **My Book**

A friend in need, Mary Brown: A NOVELLA (The Mary Brown novels Book 7)

Link: **My Book**

Dog Days for Mary Brown: A NOVELLA (The Mary Brown novels Book 8)

Link: **My Book**

Don't Mention The Hen Weekend: A Mary Brown Novel (The Mary Brown novels Book 9)

Link: **My Book**

The St. Lucia Mystery (The Mary Brown novels Book 10) -

Link: **https://amzn.to/3yFHxD8**

We'll Always Have Paris (book 11)

Link: https:/amzn.to/3Yzs02z

She's stolen my Baby (book 12)

Link: **https://amzn.to/3WS79WJ**

All the books together:

https://www.amazon.co.uk/.../Bernice-Bloom/author/ B01MPZ5SBA

Printed in Great Britain
by Amazon